SAVED BY HIS HOOD LOVE: A HOOD ROMANCE Part 2

BY

A.Lana

Saved by his hood love 2

<u>A Message From The Author</u>

Toxic people will never change. Don't let them bitches fool you. Once they show you who they are, stay away.

One must not take the simple things for granted. Never in a million years would I have thought I'd lose those I held dear and near, let alone my freedom. The snakes are out. Just make sure your grass is cut so at least you can see them. Stay woke.
 —Aaliyah

I'm tired of trying to be a good person and make the right choices. I've earned the right to be selfish. I'm going to do what I want to do. I'm not living my life afraid of what others think of me. There are no rules when it comes to making sure I'm straight, so if I gotta do something that society deems scandalous—so–damn–what. I'm putting myself first. Me over everybody.
 —Tokyo

Secrets are revealed and heartbreak and depression are lingering around.
Aaliyah was arrested for something she didn't do. Tokyo is doing her and doesn't care who she hurts. She's determined to get what she wants, even if that means crossing her blood. Jersey feels bad for Aaliyah but feels it's not his fault she's down. He's living his life and making plans to move away from Cali soon. The drama is non-stop, and the heat gets turned up in Saved By His Hood Love 2!

You never know how strong you are until being strong is the only choice you have.

"If I get a long bid, I can't be there for either one of my kids."

Jersey

"How in the fuck did the drugs get in her car?" I yelled at Tokyo.

Pacing her and Aaliyah's living room floor, I tried my best to calm down. It was hard. I was more scared than a bitch. Aaliyah got gaffled when the cops found drugs in her whip. I would have never thought no shit like that would've happened to her.

The last text I received from her was that she made it to the school, and she would call me when she left. I was so caught up in what I was doing that I hadn't even noticed it was going on at six o'clock and still hadn't heard from my girl. I tried calling her, but her phone went straight to voicemail. I couldn't ignore my gut feeling. Deep down, I knew something wasn't right. Aaliyah always answered my calls. The first thing that came to mind was that she got twisted up in my shit with Buddha. He knew more about her than I thought. He knew where she stayed and what school she attended. Aaliyah told me how he stepped to her at the club. That nigga was grimy, and hurting Aaliyah because of me was something I wouldn't put past him. I had already given him half of his money. I called the nigga Buddha.When he answered, I let him know that I would have the rest of his money by morning, and he asked me to call him then. The nigga hung up in my face. During our brief conversation, I could sense that he wasn't on no bullshit. Plus, he wouldn't be scared to let me know he had my bitch.

I didn't know what the fuck was going on, so after I finished handling business, I went to her crib. That's when I found out my girl, my baby momma, was arrested. The news felt like a ton of bricks hit me in the chest. I panicked. I could hear my own heartbeat as tiny beads of sweat trickled from my forehead.

"She probably was getting them out of the house. She tried before, but I stopped her. I told her to leave your stuff alone. She claimed that she didn't want to be a part of what you had going on. I should have told you." Tokyo explained.

She rubbed her hand down the side of my face. I knocked her hand away and stood there with an annoyed expression. "She told me about that. So, why all of a sudden she messed with it? She ain't ever messed with it before." I was all up in Tokyo's face reading her bitch ass. "Did you have something to do with this shit?"

"What?" Tokyo yelled.   Then the hoe smacked me upside the head. I wanted to hit her back, but I was already fighting a domestic violence charge fucking around with her.

"How in the hell would I have something to do with her having drugs in the car?" I began to pace back and forth again. I didn't know what the hell Aaliyah was thinking.

"Babe, just sit down. I need you to calm down. Let me fix you a drink." Tokyo offered.

I had my back towards her. I was paranoid as fuck and nervous. I didn't want Aaliyah locked up, but I wasn't trying to go either.

"I hope she don't snitch. I can't go to jail." I mumbled.

Aaliyah's momma had money and I was sure Aaliyah had a healthy savings. On top of her wealth, she was a good girl. A soon-to-be college graduate with no record and an exceptional character background. All of that should've worked in her favor.

"Thanks." I said to Tokyo. She handed me my second glass of Hennessy and a little bag of coke. After taking it to the head in one big ass gulp, I opened the baggy. I used my pinky nail to scoop up the powder. I slightly tilted my head back with my finger in my nose and sniffed it until the burning sensation hit. I felt satisfaction when I tasted it in my throat. Gotdamn, that shit was fire!

Tokyo sat next to me on the couch. I tensed up when she rubbed up and down my back.

"So, are you going to go down there and tell them that those drugs belong to you?"

My head snapped to the side, gawking at her. I was trying to figure out if she was crazy or dumb as hell. It felt like the bitch was trying to be funny.

"I can help you with a lawyer. How many strikes do you have?"

I was feeling some type of way from the word lawyer, the mention of me having strikes, and the thought of going to prison for a very long time. It caused my stomach to ball up in a knot. I shook my head and let out a long sigh.

"If I say it's mine, those white folks are going to throw the book at me. If she takes the rap, the most she will get is probation."

"You want her to take the charge?" Tokyo's eyes bucked. "What about the baby?" She quickly asked.

"How do you know she is pregnant?" From what I knew, Aaliyah hadn't announced it. She wanted to wait until she was at least four months.

"She is my sister." Tokyo snapped.

I stared at her in deep thought. This shit was wild. I had to figure out my next move.

"That's another thing she will have on her side, the baby in her stomach."

"Look, I can't communicate with her. I know she will say something over the phone that she isn't supposed to. If I get a long bid, I can't be there for either one of my kids."
That shit was true.
Tokyo placed her hand on her tummy.
"Don't worry. I will figure this out. I love you, Jersey. I got you. Me and the baby need you. Despite what you think, I love my sister too. Me, my mother, and her mother will handle it." She assured.
I sat there staring at Tokyo. Maybe she wasn't the evil bitch I thought she was. This situation showed another side of her. Giving her a head nod, I stood up from the couch.
"Where are you going?" She asked, standing up with me.
"To lay low for a little bit. I will keep in touch." I leaned down and kissed her.
"Call me." She pleaded.
"I promise." With that, I walked out the door.

"I don't care how educated she is, I'll always label her as dumb."

Tokyo

Soooo the bitch thought she was just going to mess up my life by telling my man I had an abortion and in return, he left me. Now he's dead, and she's to blame for it. If we were together, the cops probably would have never gotten a chance to kill him. That bitch Aaliyah ran her big mouth to my man about me getting an abortion and I lost my first love. Now I'm expected to let her and Jersey live happily ever after with their baby and the money she was getting from Dad's estate. Ha! That wouldn't be happenin' as long as I'm breathing. I don't care how educated she is, I'll always label her as dumb. Book sense, but no common sense. When it comes to Jersey the girl is stupid, but she knows she's stupid and that almost makes her smart. She is supposed to be my sister, but the sneaky tramp never told me about the baby or the money she would inherit.

As my momma said, she's a grimy hoe. She had to be dealt with family or not. She was telling me to get revenge, and that is what I did. Some may call me scandalous, but at the end of the day, I don't give a fuck. I don't care about anybody who doesn't care about me. So, don't judge me, just mind your business.

Aaliyah told me she was going to bed early. I guess the pregnancy had her sleepy. I was in my feelings. Furthermore, I was going to call Jersey and cuss him the fuck out, but I didn't. I rolled myself a fat blunt while sitting in my beautiful backyard drinking on Patron while plotting my revenge. After my third drink, I came up with the perfect idea. Around two o'clock in the morning, I crept into Aaliyah's room, grabbed two duffle bags out of her closet, and ran into my room. Only one bag had drugs. My pussy got wet thinking how I was about to ruin my snake ass sister's life. To make sure Jersey wasn't near, I called him, and he sent me to voicemail. I texted.

Me: The baby is hungry.

Baby Daddy: Man, Door Dash it. I'm working.

Instead of responding, I sneaked Aaliyah's keys and put the drugs in her car. Then I went into the backyard and called Parker. Parker is a cop who also has a fetish for men. Jersey and I hooked up with him several times. I knew that I would need to use him one day, and this was the day.

"Come to my house. We need to talk. Now!" I hung up. He knew not to fuck with me because I had threatened him before. There was one particular day that Jersey and I wanted to play, but he preferred to spend time with his wife. I could have let him, but I chose to pull my pimp card. I sent him a video of us with a caption that read, "Our little secret." He read right in between the lines and showed up to play with Jersey and I that night.

What I wanted happened, and Parker showed up. I told him what I needed him to do. The next morning, Aaliyah left for school. I called the police station with a tip, and they arrested her at the school. Parker was the detective on the scene who was assigned to the case. He would make sure the charges stuck like glue.

"Girl, what are you over here thinking about?" My momma asked. I was in her backyard having a cocktail, daydreaming about the future Jersey and I would have now that Aaliyah was out of the way.
She took a seat next to me and crossed her legs.
"Thinking about Aaliyah, and the baby she is carrying."
"Well, that ain't your problem. She don't care about you, Tokyo. I don't even know

why you give a fuck. Her big refrigerator body ass has always thought she was better than you were, just like her damn mammy." She paused for a brief moment. "You know she's dying." She mentioned with no remorse. She crossed her legs and fired up an apple flavored Black & Mild.

My eyes grew bigger than a full moon. My heart dropped and knees trembled. I couldn't believe Ms. Lori was dying. I was now a nervous wreck.

"No, I didn't know. How did you find out?"

"She called me today crying about her daughter. She had been leaving me messages, but I never called her back. I knew why she was calling. She better be glad Warren had just ate me out and gave me a few stacks. I was in a good mood. That is the only reason I answered." She inhaled the cigar smoke and blew it out in my direction causing a smoke cloud to form around me.

"What did she say? How is she dying? Oh my God." I fanned the smoky cloud away while still feeling saddened about the news.

My momma whipped her head to the side, and intentionally blew smoke smack in my face.

"Bitch, why do you care? Acting too much like you give a fuck for me."

"She raised me." I cocked my head to the side in annoyance from what she was doing. I stared at her for a brief moment. She could be so disrespectful at times.

I mean, I didn't hate Ms. Lori. I just didn't like her because Daddy felt like her and Aaliyah were better than Momma and me. I didn't want her to die.

"Well, call the half dead hoe." Momma spat.

"Damn, Momma. You hate her that much that you're wishing death on her?" I shook my head.

"Damn, Tokyo. You want a nigga that bad you would set your own sister up, and now she won't be here when her momma dies or to raise her child." She snapped back.

My mouth dropped. My mother's statement appalled me. This bitch was feeling herself. Damn, I thought I was evil. This bitch was The Seed of Chucky.

"I see." I stood up. "Can't trust you, either. Why in the fuck you bring that up? Nita's man is giving you money. So, don't play like you give a fuck about me to get in my pockets."

I was far from stupid. I knew my mother didn't give a fuck about me like she put on. My momma was an opportunist. All she cared about was what she could get. Now that she had a nigga breaking her off, she wanna act like she's the shit.

Patricia stood up. We were eye to eye. I hoped she knew that she didn't pump no fear in my heart. I couldn't believe I confided in her and told her what I did. That was so stupid on my part. Never again.

"You better watch who the fuck you're talking to. This is my gotdamn house, and I pay the bills up in here. Girl, your little money ain't doing shit."

"Oh, since you fucking Auntie Nita's man, you wanna say my money ain't shit."

"Girl, I can fuck Nita's man, your broke ass man, and whoever else's. He don't want Nita's ass just like Jersey don't want you." She spat. She paused for a minute. "Hell, I'd rather commit suicide than to fuck that sorry muthafucka you laying down with. He ain't worth a bucket of shit."

Yeah, she was feeling herself. I rolled my eyes up towards the sky. The woman was talking crazy as hell.

"Bitch, what in the fuck did you just say?" Our necks snapped towards the unexpected voice. Nita stormed our way. She was burning mad with smoke shooting from her ears. Momma popped up from the chair, staring with one hand on her hip like she double dared her to do something.

Wham! With an open hand, Nita slapped Momma so hard her drawstring ponytail flew off. I stepped backwards. Any other time I would have jumped in to help her, but she was talking big shit so she needed her ass beat. I wanted Nita to whoop her ass like she was a disobedient child.

"Bitch, I know you didn't put your damn hands on me!" Momma screamed out.

She raised her leg like The Matrix, kicking Nita so hard she flew backwards. Momma raced over, grabbed a handful of her hair, and snatched her wig off exposing her thin cornrows braided to the back.

"Baldhead, bitch!" Momma name-called while twirling the wig high in the air. Without warning, Momma pulled her pants down, smacked herself on the ass, and rubbed the wig between her legs and tossed it in Nita's face. "Now, go ask your man if your wig smells like my pussy. He knows because he keeps his head down here." She pointed right at her kitty.

Nita's lip curled and face frowned. I knew things were about to get even uglier. She popped Momma in the face with a two-piece, knocking her to the ground and right on her ass. She jumped on top of her and began raining blows to Momma's face.

"Get this bitch off me!" Momma screamed to the top of her lungs.

I stood there for a minute. See, her mouth had written a check that her ass couldn't cash. However, she was still my momma. I pushed and tugged at Nita until I got her off of her.

"That's enough. Don't hit her again." I warned with a balled fist. I didn't want to go there with my aunt, but if I had to I would without hesitation.

"Oh y'all bitches wanna jump me?" Nita swung on me. That bitch hit me in the head so hard I caught an instant headache. I swear I saw stars, Jupitar, and Mars. When I fell, she stomped me. I knew I had to fight back. I hopped up like a bunny rabbit and started swinging on her. I socked her with a hard left that sent her straight to the ground. I didn't know where Momma went with her trifling ass. Auntie Nita balled into a fetal position, covering her face. I stopped fighting. I felt sympathy for her. I didn't want to hit her, but she pushed me to the limit.

POW POW... the gunshots that went off caused me to take off running for my life. I didn't know what was going on.

"Bitch, get your stupid ass out of my yard. Yeah, I'm fucking Warren. That's your dumb ass fault. You are the one who wanted to have a threesome, knowing your pussy wack."

I peeped from the side of the house when I heard Momma talking. That shit had me throwed off when I learned Momma and Nita were having threesomes. Freaky asses. Nita slowly got up from the ground and stood there looking like a furious bull. My face stung. I could feel blood running down the side of my head. Truth be told, Auntie Nita hit harder than Mike Tyson. That woman was no joke.

'Ohhhh, I can lie and tell Jersey I had a miscarriage because that bitch stomped me out.' I thought to myself.

"I came over here to tell my best friend how I got a disease from the nigga." She laughed. "You probably gave it to him. Those probably were your dirty ass panties I saw in his truck. You trifling, hoe."
"I know you better get out of my yard."
"Every time I see you, I am going to beat your ass. You and your trifling ass daughter will never have good luck." She slid her foot out of her shoe and threw it at me. It hit me right in the head. I swooped it up from the ground and swung it right back. She ducked. "You missed, bitch!"
 She grabbed her shoe from the street, put it on her foot, and stormed off. I wondered what all she heard. I felt dizzy. Momma shouldn't have repeated that shit. I bet Nita heard her telling my business too.

"My life was over."
Aaliyah

2 months later

"Momma." I sobbed with a stream of tears flowing down my face. "I know I ain't supposed to cry in a place like this but what the fuck, Momma. 15 years?" I stood in the cell on the dirty ass payphone, crying to my mother. I was sentenced less than an hour ago. My life was over for some shit I didn't even do. I had never cussed in front of my mother but what I was feeling, I wanted to spazz on the world.

"I know, baby, we should have just taken the deal." She cried while trying to get her coughing under control.

The deal was five years. I didn't feel I should have pleaded guilty when the drugs weren't mine. Now I regretted it. A whole ten extra years. 27 years old, serving a 15-year bid because a man I loved and whom I thought loved me left his drugs in my car. Why in the hell was he in my car, anyway? I had no clue. He never used my car. He always said it's too girly and by him being in the streets he didn't want people knowing his girl's car. I couldn't figure out what changed.

"Mommy, I don't think I can make it." I cried like a baby. I didn't give a damn who heard me. Or what they thought of me. I

21

knew one damn thing, if anyone tried to test me because they looked at me as weak, I was going to take all of my frustration out on them. I swear I could see myself killing a person with my bare hands. "This isn't fair." I wept as I stomped my feet.

"Please don't cry. Aaliyah, you are stronger than you think you are." My mother said. I don't know why she even thought that because I was weak ass fuck. What I had to go through would bring the toughest person to their knees. My life was over.

"Mom, I'm pregnant. I can't have my baby here."

"Ohhhh, Aaliyah. I will do whatever I have to do to get you out." She promised.

Sometime later

"Momma doesn't think I should adopt Tokyo's baby, but I want to." I said to my cousin Mona. We sat in the living room having cocktails and finger foods. We were back talking, but I still felt some kind of way about her.

"Do you want the baby because it is your niece, and you don't want her in the system, or is it because Jersey asked you to get the baby?"

Picking up my drink from the table, I cut my eyes at Mona before taking a sip. I don't know why she assumed I would take on the responsibility of raising a child just to keep a man.

'Ugly, bitch. Always got something to say with her four baby daddies'. I said in my head.

"So you think I am that in love with Jersey that I would take on the role of raising a child. Mind you, I will be putting my life on hold doing this. No, I love my niece and that is the least I can do." I said, feeling a little sick to my stomach. Every time I thought about what took place almost nine months ago, I felt uneasy. Something was telling me it would backfire.

"If you are doing it from the heart and not because the nigga asked you to or because you feel guilty about being with your sister's man, then go for it." She gulped down the drink in her cup before standing up.

"I gotta use it, and bitch don't look at me like that."

"I can do what the hell I want to do. You always got some shit to say like you ain't ever fucked another bitch's man. The difference between me and you is the nigga is still with me."

Mona walked up to me. I stared up at her ghetto ass. Hoping she didn't hit me upside the head like she would do when we were younger, and I got smart.

"The difference between you and me is, I may fuck other bitches' men, but I ain't ever betrayed my blood. I don't do bitches like you. I love your black ass because we are family, and that's the only reason why I fuck with you."

After speaking her mind, she walked off. Crossing one leg over the other, I finished my drink. I truly did want custody of my niece because I loved her and didn't want her in the system. I promised myself that I would treat my niece as my own.

Thinking about the shit Mona said had me hot. Her admitting that she doesn't do bitches like me had me salty. What the fuck does she mean she only deals with me because I'm her cousin? Ok, broke hoe. I had a trick for her ass. I logged out of my Instagram account and logged into my fake page. I then located Oscar, her baby daddy. Oscar was a baller out of Las Vegas. He cheated on his girl with Mona and got her pregnant. The only reason she kept the baby is that Oscar is paid. One night, Mona, Aunt Nita, Momma, and I had a girl's night. Mona thought we were sleeping. I heard her confess to my momma how Little Oscar's daddy wasn't the nigga who paid her child support every month and let her and her kids live in that nice house she stayed in. It didn't surprise me when I overheard Momma encourage her to keep milking the nigga until she couldn't anymore. Well, I hoped the bitch had money saved.

Me: Little Oscar is not your son. That is your cousin's baby. They are both playing you. Get a blood test and thank me later. You'll finally get rid of the bitch.

Shrugging my shoulders, I logged out with a devious smile on my face.

All I knew was that everybody had better stop playing with me like their shit didn't stink. I'm just the bitch to put you out there.

A dog will look down when he has done wrong, a snake will look you right in your eyes. -

> "People are users, narcissists, and
> opportunists."

<u>Val</u>

"I can't wait to see who her baby daddy is. She has been keeping that a secret." My cousin Snow admitted.

She grabbed the gift bag sitting by her door. I scooped up the box of pampers that I was giving the hoe. We headed to Tokyo's baby shower.

"We will see. I can't wait to see the expression on that bitch's face when I come walking in behind you." I looked at Snow and she shook her head. My cousin could've passed for a younger version of the R&B singer Ciara. She was beautiful. I didn't understand why she was so insecure about being thin.

"Don't get us put out." She advised, and then laughed.

"I can't promise you that." I hit the lock on my Range Rover and the both of us climbed in on our respectful sides. The moment the car started, 'Rich Nigga' by Pretty Uno blared from the speakers.

When Snow told me that Tokyo invited her to the baby shower, I invited myself. Snow knew I intended to be on some other shit. Tokyo only showed up to one of Aaliyah's court dates. I reached out to the hoe when I got the news about Aaliyah's mom

27

passing, and she never got back to me. I knew it was depressing for Aaliyah. I knew my best friend, and losing her freedom for something I knew for a fact she didn't do broke her. It hurt that she shut me out. It didn't stop me from writing to her and praying that one day she would respond.

When we pulled in front of the mini-mansion, memories of my best friend hit me and caused me to tear up. My girl was gone for fifteen years. I didn't have any proof, but I knew that Jersey had something to do with those drugs being in her car. The fact that he didn't show up to court spoke volumes.

The block was packed with cars. People were walking up with gifts. After searching for about five minutes, we found a parking spot further down the block. Lucky for us, we dressed comfortably. Snow rocked a blue hip hugging Maxi dress with a white shirt tied around her waist to match her white Dior sneakers. I wore an Off-White T-shirt, a pair of Off-White biker shorts, and Off-White sneakers. I already knew I was coming to be on bullshit so instead of wearing a purse I wore my Gucci fanny pack. With designer shades covering my eyes, my cousin and I walked down the street.

I was in deep thought. At 25, I finally realized that I couldn't expect people to treat me the way I treated them. I treated people right, but most didn't return the love. People were selfish; they only cared about themselves. If they couldn't benefit from you or as soon as you start calling them on their bullshit, you are labeled the bad person. Well, that's how I felt. I was so sick of selfish people, I swear.

"What you thinking about, cousin?"

"I'm thinking about how genuine Aaliyah is. People are users, narcissists, and opportunists. Bitches be out here showing fake love acting like they care about you but be the same ones keeping your name in their mouths. I don't like all that phony shit. The main reason behind the hating is jealousy. Jealous, your light shines brighter than theirs with no effort. Real talk, these hoes don't mind you doing good as long as you're not doing better than them. Fake is the new 'real.' Muthafuckas love fake shit. Shit, your own man can be jealous of you and family ain't no better." I shook my head in disgust.

Snow turned to face me. She nodded her head in agreement.

"That is so true, cousin. It's sad. Jersey is a lame for not stepping up. Have you seen him?"

"He's more than a lame. He's a bitch ass nigga. I ain't seen him, though. I know I can't whoop a nigga but if I see him, I swear I'm going to try to beat his ass."

From my peripheral, I could see Snow shaking her head.
"It's sad that she lost her mother while in prison. I hope she doesn't go crazy in there."
"I wish that she would write me back. At least let me be there for her."
"I will be praying for her. I will have Momma put her on the prayer list at church." That's how we found out Ms. Lori passed. She used to be a member at Snow's church before she moved to the A.
"Thanks, cousin."
 When we approached the gate, we entered through the driveway. There were beautiful purple, pink, and white balloon garlands that spelled out the words WELCOME BABY DREAM. This bitch was doing the most.

"Dream. Wow. Aaliyah would always say if she had a girl, she would name her Dream. That bitch is a hater." I spat. Cutting my eyes at the décor, Snow and I made our way around the circular driveway and into the back of the yard.
"Damn, done stole the girl's baby's name." Snow scoffed.

When we made it to the backyard, I admired the pretty decorations. It was a Caribbean themed baby shower with a touch of Disneyland. Six large artificial palm trees lined the center of the yard. Next to each tree stood gigantic stuffed Disney characters. The party decorator placed pineapple and coconut décor on each table and mini waterfall centerpieces. Customized tablecloths with the name **DREAM** monogrammed in a fancy font covered the tables. There were at least forty tables out there. Off to the side was a 360-photo booth. Alongside it was an extra-long food table filled with elegant platters of chicken quesadillas, chicken spring rolls, coconut shrimp, sausage cheddar-balls, mini-pizzas, mini cheesecakes, shrimp cocktail, and ham and cheese sandwiches. Two servers stood behind it wearing aprons and gloves. To the right of it, I spotted an enormous sized pink and white Minnie Mouse cake.

Disneyland costume characters dressed as Minnie Mouse, Mickey Mouse, Tinkerbell, Peter Pan, Cinderella, and Disney Princess pranced around greeting and waving at the adults and children that arrived as guests.

"It's nice." Snow admitted as we set our gifts on the gift table.

"I agree." I replied, cutting my eyes.

I looked around to see if I spotted Tokyo. When I saw a decorated king and queen chair, I was eager to see who her baby daddy was.

Snow and I mingled. Tokyo had quite a few local celebrities in the building. Being that I knew alot of people in the music industry, the faces were very familiar. The Disney Princess's performance overflowed with cuteness. Aaliyah loved Disney. I couldn't help but to think that Tokyo wanted to steal her sister's life.

Envious, bitch.

An hour later, the DJ spoke. "The parents will be making their entrance shortly. Until then, I want you all to keep dancing and enjoying yourselves."

"If you are standing, please stand by your seats or find a spot on each side of the red carpet." Pat, Tokyo's mother loudly slurred with a glass of red wine in her hand. Apparently, she couldn't hold her liquor. "If you can't do what I tell you to do, take your black funky asses home." She rudely insulted.

Nobody paid her any attention because that was normal behavior for her crazy butt.

Tokyo and her mother were twins. She was dressed in a tight-fit white mini dress wearing open-toe high heels, which showed off her blue polished toenails. I couldn't help but frown in disappointment at her. Her unsupportive ass only showed up on Aaliyah's sentencing day.

Britney Spears' song titled 'My Baby' played through the huge speakers.

"Tiny hands/Yes, that's you/And all you show/It's simply true/I smell your breath/It makes me cry/I wonder how I've lived my life..." Britney sweetly sang.

The crowd started to ohh and ahhhh. I saw Snow turn to look, but I did the opposite. I looked straight ahead until I had to look.

A white pony pulled a carriage holding a car seat. I'm thinking to myself, *She already had the baby.* I looked up, and my eyes could have popped out of my head. Jersey escorted Tokyo in. My heart rate increased as my nose flared. My eyebrows scrunched together. I gawked at the couple. I could barely control my breathing. I was so angry. I balled both fists up. I could feel my blood boiling. I didn't know what the fuck was going on. I stomped their way.

"Girl." Snow whispered.

She grabbed me by the arm, pulling me back. I was seconds away from confronting both of them.

"Not now. They ain't going to do nothing but put you out."

"I don't give a fuck. This ain't only fucked up, but sick. Bitch, I am about to lose it." I warned.

I felt people staring at me. I didn't give two flying fucks. This was some scandalous shit.

"Fuck it." Snow said.

She knew me all too well and no matter if she disagreed with my bullshit, she had my back.

"I'm on whatever you on. Bitch, we're outnumbered, but it's whatever." My eyes were glued on the grimy couple.

"I can understand how you feel. Aaliyah is cool. That's that bitch's sister."

The disloyal trifling couple made it to their seats, and everyone clapped. Pat took the baby from the carriage and handed her to Tokyo, ignoring Jersey who had his arms held out.

I faced Snow.

"You know what? Let's go because I swear it's going to get ugly if I stay." I cautioned.

I had a baby of my own at home. I couldn't risk getting locked up. I wouldn't hear the end of the shit. Plus, my child needed me.

"Yeah, let's go." Snow agreed.

We turned and headed for the exit. However, I just couldn't leave without giving them a piece of my mind. I wouldn't be a good friend if I didn't say a word.

Marching over to where scandalous 1 and 2 were, I stood in front of Tokyo. I was itching to knock the frown off the bitch's face.

"Can I help you?" She sassed, looking me up and down.

"No bitch, you can't. So what you on? You got a baby by your sister's man."

"Val, this is me and Aaliyah's baby." Jersey responded. "Tokyo got custody of her, so she wouldn't go to the system. You're tripping."

"Don't explain shit to her. Why are you here? You were not invited." Tokyo raised her voice a notch.

"Why? You didn't want me to see you with your sister's man? Playing house?"

I didn't care what Jersey said. The shit was suspect to me.

"It ain't like that." Jersey retorted. "Aaliyah had my baby while she was in jail."

I looked at the beautiful baby in Tokyo's arm and saw Aaliyah's entire face. My eyes began to water. I fought hard not to shed a tear.

"Jersey, stop explaining to her. Let her think what she wants." She suddenly looked at me. "Get the fuck out of my shower before I have you arrested for trespassing."

I stared at Jersey.

"You let your baby momma go to jail for some shit that wasn't even hers. Nigga, karma is a bitch." I then looked at Tokyo. "You are one hateful evil bitch. The devil. You didn't even support your sister. Not one time, hoe."

"I was there the first day, but that is none of your business. Mom, throw this wife of a crackhead out of my shower!" She yelled. I had to chuckle to keep from going nuts. Muthafuckas were always trying to throw what Tiger did in my face like it was supposed to hurt me.

"Let's go, cuz. It ain't worth it." Snow grabbed my hand. I gave them one last stare before I stormed off. As I walked away, suddenly I felt cold liquid splash against the back of my head. I touched the back of my neck. It was red wine seeping down from it. Pat stood there staring at me. The woman had tossed wine on me.

"Get the fuck away from here before I break my shoe off in your ass!" She threatened. I broke towards her, but a few tall stout women who looked like dudes whisked me up like a light feather.

"My auntie told you to take your ass on." One of the lesbians dressed in men's attire growled as she tightly gripped me under the arm, ushering me out of the party. Snow fast paced right behind us.

There was no way we would go head up with three chicks built like linebackers. Hell to the NO!

"If she wants to fight, hit that bitch so hard that she lands in Japan. When she wakes up, she'll be speaking Japanese!" Pat hollered out to her nieces. The guests burst out into a fit of laughter. I was hot as fish grease. That bitch threw wine on me. I promised on my life if I ever saw her without them manly bitches, I was going to jail for assault. I was gon' whoop her old ass. And that's on gang!

"So, what do you think about that shit?" Snow asked.

I stared at the red light. When it turned green, I mashed on the gas. My feelings were hurt. Aaliyah was like the coolest, most humble person I could've ever met. For them to fuck over her like that pissed me off. For the people I love, I am very overprotective.

"I think they are fucking and using my friend's baby to make their family. I know they are." The tears I had been holding in trickled from my eyes. "I can't believe she was pregnant. I wonder if she knew before she was arrested or found out in jail. Oh my God, Snow. She had to go through that all alone. Losing her mom, being arrested for something she didn't do and on top of that having a baby alone. A baby she had to give up."

I slammed my hand on the steering wheel. That was so jacked up. Thinking about my friend suffering in that fucked up place crushed me.

"I swear, I will be praying hard for her." Snow promised.

The rest of the ride was silent. When I pulled up to Snow's, I threw the truck in park.

"You wanna come in and have a drink?" She offered.

"Nah. I wanna hug my baby. Maybe take him to the park."

"K." She put her hand on my lap. "Try not to let this get you in a funk. I know how hard you love. Just don't worry yourself but pray. God still answers prayers, you know."

"I know." I replied somberly.

"Hug?" She asked. Turning in our seats, we hugged.

"I love you, cousin."

"I love you too, Val."

Snow's mom and my dad were twins. She was five years younger than me, but even at 20 she was very mature and one of my favorite people to hang out with. Besides Aaliyah, she was the one I confided in.

"I'm glad you are home." Snow moved back to Cali after living in New York for two years. I had a feeling that her free-spirited ass would be leaving again.

"So am I."

 She grabbed her purse and climbed out of the truck.

When I pulled out of the parking lot, I thought about going home, but I decided to go have drinks at Ruth Chris. If I wasn't in my feelings, I would have invited Snow, but I just wanted to be alone. Luckily, I had a blazer in the truck to put on, covering up the back of my wine-stained shirt.

I knew the general manager, so not having a reservation didn't stop me from dining in. The waitress escorted me to a seat. Immediately, I ordered a drink. I needed one badly. Not only did Jersey and Tokyo have me heated, but I had other stuff going on in my life too. My baby's daddy was an embarrassment. All the blogs talked about was him doing drugs, me writing his music, and the anonymous baby mama he so-called had. I prayed hard for a way out. If it wasn't for our son, I would've been gone.

In deep thought, I scanned the restaurant and was caught by surprise when I saw Jam and a little girl dining not too far from me. Jam was the white boy I met out with Aaliyah one night. We ended up being cool and clicked instantly. His white ass switched up on me, and I had no idea why. I wasn't going to ask, either. Low-key, I did

feel some kind of way. He was like a breath
of fresh air.

Flashback

Me: Hey.
Jam: *What's up, pretty?*

*I blushed. He called me that the first day
we met.*

*I was surprised that he texted back. I
reached out to him two months prior
several times, and he never hit me back. I
felt some kind of way when I was out with
Tiger — The next day after I text him and
saw him up in his section with a bitch on
his lap, I hadn't texted the nigga since. The
day Aaliyah was sentenced, he was the
person my heart desired. I didn't know why,
but I reached out.*

Me: *I need you. A friend. I'm so hurt.*

*Seconds later, my phone began to ring. It
was Jam.*

*"Hi." I spoke just above a whisper. It was
my way of preventing me from breaking
down again.*

"Where are you?" He asked. I could hear dudes laughing and talking loud in the background.

"If you're busy, I can call you another time."

"Pretty, where are you? You're trying to talk low. You've been crying?"

"Yes. I'm sitting in the parking lot of the Criminal Court building. My best friend was just sentenced to fifteen years." I sobbed into the phone.

"Damn. I'm sorry. Send me your location. I'm on the way."

I managed to pull myself together long enough to share my location. With my head back, I cried. I sobbed so hard that I could feel my body shaking. My home girl didn't deserve that. With my head back on the seat, I tried to get myself together.

"You, ok?" His voice was followed by a cool breeze. I must've forgotten to lock my door. My eyes popped open, and I looked at him. Even in my distraught state, I couldn't help but notice how fine Mr. Vanilla was.

"This is so fucked up." I cried.

Jam pulled my body towards him. I wrapped my arms around his neck, and he scooped me into his arms.

"I brought the homie with me. He is going to drive your car to my house." He walked me over to his car. The door was open, and he easily placed me in the passenger seat.

"Is it cool if my boy drives your car?"
I nodded my head yes.
"I got your purse and phone. Anything else you need?"
I shook my head no.
Jam shut the door. By the time he made it back in the car, I was crying again. Not only for Aaliyah, but also for myself. Jam was a stranger, and he showed me more compassion than Tiger had done in months. Tiger didn't even give a fuck about my friend, if you asked me.
"That's what goes on when you mess with dope dealers." Tiger had the audacity to say.
"And what happens when you mess with dope heads?" I snapped.
Tiger left the room, calling me ignorant in the process. The more I tried with him, the more I wanted to say fuck whatever it was that we had going on. The way Jam came to my rescue and showed that he cared

about my well-being touched me in more ways than he could've ever imagined.

Once we arrived at his place, a very nice house I might add, he turned to me.
"I share this home with my boys. Only my homie Yogi, who drove your car back, is here."

"That's fine. I hope you have something for a headache."

"Depending on what you wanna take?" He smirked before winking. I caught him eying me while biting his bottom lip.

"Do I need to carry you inside?"

"Yes." I smiled. Why not get treated like a queen. With my eyes closed, I laid my head on his hard chest and trusted wherever it was he was taking me.

When I opened my eyes, I was being placed on a smoky grey colored round sofa. It sat in front of a picture window. The view of the waterfall and the man-made pond was breathtaking.
"I'll be right back." I looked at Jam, and he gave me an assuring smile. I watched him as he headed out of the bedroom door. His

room wasn't as big as the room I shared with my baby's daddy, but it was a nice size. A typical bachelor's room. California king-size bed, two nightstands, and a 72-inch flat-screen on the wall. There were a couple of paintings on the wall but apart from that, it was neat and basic.

Looking back out the window, I daydreamed about several things. My friend, my happiness, and my depression. Also, I thought about my relationship with Tiger and our son. So many things had me in deep thought. I didn't even notice Jam when he walked back in.

"I got some things I thought you may need during a time like this." I turned at the sound of his voice. In front of me was a tray. On it was a bowl of fruit, a pack of crackers, two bottles of Fiji water, a cognac glass half-filled with ice, and a bottle of Remy.

"Thank you so much." I reached for the glass. Jam grabbed the Remy bottle and after opening it, he poured me some. Pulling a bottle of Tylenol from his pocket, he handed it to me.

"You free to kick it here for however long you like. I was playing basketball when you called me. I'm about to take a shower."

That's when I noticed him in his gray sweat shorts and a white T-shirt.

"You see something you like?"
I smirked before taking my eyes off the budge showing through in his shorts.
"Don't believe that bullshit."
"What bullshit?" I asked, truly puzzled.
"White boys got little dicks." He grabbed himself. Blushing, I turned my head, looking back out the window. The boy's dick was huge, and he wasn't even hard.
"Thanks for being a friend."
"You got that." Jam had walked up to me. I looked at him and he kissed my forehead. I didn't know if I was just vulnerable or he was doing some things to make me desire him. He showered and came back about thirty-minutes later.

"Take your street clothes off and lay with me. I promise I won't try anything." I glanced up.

What if I want you too, I thought. Not giving it a second thought, I stood up feeling a little tipsy. I took off my skirt and shirt. Dressed in a silk camisole set, I made my way to the other side of the bed.
I told him all about Aaliyah being sentenced.

"Jersey's girl is the one who got sentenced today, right?"

"That's not his girl. He should've taken his case. Aaliyah isn't lying, she didn't do shit."

"That's some fucked up shit. I ain't seen that nigga in a minute. Scary ass probably skipped town."

"I hope he dies." I admitted.

That night, Jam and I talked. I mean like a real-life conversation. It wasn't one of those one-sided conversations like I had whenever I tried to talk to Tiger. Jam talked back. He had an opinion and offered suggestions. I would have moments where I would think of Aaliyah and her losing her freedom and I would cry. Jam held me tight. It was the affection, the communication, and the bomb ass head that had me thinking whatever it was that was brewing between us would become something we both would enjoy sipping. That was seven months ago and I ain't heard from him since.

Seeing him tonight in the restaurant with the little girl I figured she and her mother were the reason I hadn't heard from him. I couldn't be mad at that. Disappointed and hurt maybe because I thought we were friends but not mad.

"Thank you." I smiled at the waitress when she handed me my drink. I looked up and Jam was staring at me. Never the one to show I'm pressured, I flashed him a smile with a cute wave. Taking a sip from my drink, I focused on my phone. What a day.

Seeing Val's pretty ass wasn't something I was trying to do right then. To keep it real, I was trying to avoid her. During the short period we kicked it and talked on the phone, I felt comfortable with her. She was like a home girl I was crushing on. I allowed her to do most of the talking. I was never the one to open up, but Val made it easy to share a few of my feelings with her. I told her, not knowing my parents left me guarded and unable to trust. Nevertheless, I was grateful I had my mom. She didn't have to step up and take me in, but she did. That's the most I shared about my feelings. I found myself caring about hers. It was weird and felt foreign. Val was a stranger, but I fucked with her the long way, she just didn't know.

"I will be right back." I said, looking at my daughter and then at her mother, who had joined us for dinner. After months, I had finally let Karen see our daughter.

"Who is she? Where do you know her from?" Karen asked, looking towards Val, who was walking out the door. I put my hand up to stop her from pressing me about how I knew her. Val was known throughout the hood.

"Chill." I told her. I gave her one last look before heading out after Val. I knew I should've left well enough alone. I had too much going on to even entertain another man's woman, but it was something about her boss status. Her confidence and mean but caring spirit pulled me into her.

"Val." I called her name. She had just handed the valet her ticket.
"Hey." She mumbled.
"So you're just going to ignore me?" I asked. I was now standing next to her.

She looked at me from my Dolce sneakers up to my red A hat and then into my blue eyes.

"I spoke." She batted her eyes and then peered towards a silver colored G Wagon.

"Nice ride."

"Thanks." She headed to her car.

"It was nice seeing you." I didn't know what else to say.

"Likewise." She tossed the one-worded statement over her shoulder before dipping into her ride.

I stood there watching as she pulled off.

I sent her a text.

Me: I miss you. Sorry if I have been distant. Can we have lunch tomorrow?

I chuckled when she left me on read with no response. I wasn't ready no way.

"Real love will have you doing things you said you would never do."

Jam

1 month later

"Where is the gotdamn owner?" I heard a female's voice loudly ask. I sat in my office having lunch. I saw her on the camera when she came to get her car. I watched as she got in and waited for her to get back out. Looking at her in a one-piece short set showing off that sexy ass body of hers, my dick stiffened. Val knew she was fine as fuck. She wore a gold twist braid down to her waist. Baby girl was too sexy to me.

"What can I help you with?" The receptionist inquired.

"You can help me by getting the gotdamn manager." She replied. Loud was an understatement.
I took pride in my place of business. I would never allow a customer's voice to elevate like that but since nobody was in the shop, I sat back enjoying watching her get upset.
"What is the issue?" My receptionist asked.

"Somebody stole my damn gun and wallet out of my glove compartment. If you don't get it to me now, I swear I will blow this bitch up."

"I can assure you our workers don't steal. I apologize, but we are not responsible for stolen items. Why would you leave such items?" Ms. Jason was always so calm. Her vibe either pissed you off or calmed you down. She was pissing Val off.

"Listen, woman." Val barked.
 I could tell she was losing the little patience she had. I hurried and ran into the lobby.

"I am the owner. How can I help you?" I asked, walking up to her, never breaking our gaze. She didn't know the frown on her face turned me the fuck on. "You are asking about the owner. I am the owner." I smirked. Taking her by the hand, I pulled it to my lips and kissed it.
"Jam, I have a feeling you got something to do with my shit being taken out of my car." She narrowed her eyes on me. "That's not cool."
"I've been texting you, and you keep leaving me on read. I've been thinking about you like crazy. You are so gotdamn fine to me. When I went to inspect the car and saw your face on the ID in your wallet, I knew right then I had to get my friend back."

"So you take your customer's shit?"

"Mr. Jam, I know you are the owner, but that is not something you do to get a woman's attention. We will have to have a long talk later." My receptionist, who was my old middle school teacher, scolded. I knew I was in trouble with her. This was my detail shop, but I swear she ran the place. I wouldn't have it any other way.

"Yes, Ma'am."

"Jam, can I have my things, so I can go?" Val yanked her hand from mine.

"You think it's just a coincidence that you are walking back into my life?"

"I came to get my car detailed. One of my clients spoke highly of this place. That's it, that's all. Period."

"You gotta come to my office if you want it back." I chuckled, knowing she was mad. I turned and headed to my office. Her sassy ass was hot on my heels.

Walking over, shutting, and locking the door, I turned back around and pulled her into my arms, hugging her tightly. I could tell she wanted to be there, but she acted hard.

"Can you please let me go?"

"I'm sorry." I admitted kissing her on the side of her neck.

"What are you sorry for?" She asked.

Damn, she smelled good.

"Sorry that I stopped responding to your calls and texts. Sorry, because I felt like you wouldn't understand what I got going on in my life, so instead of keeping it real I walked away." I confessed. Val was like a breath of fresh air. I ain't ever believed in that soulmate shit. However, from day one, this woman had me feeling some shit I had never felt with any other woman.

I broke our embrace, so I could look into her eyes.

"Val, I like you. I like your vibe. You are so pretty to me. I'm flawed as fuck. Got a lot of shit going on." I admitted.

"I like you too. I have never ever been attracted to a man outside of my race. I think you are handsome. Your blonde hair, blue eyes and swag turns me on." She smirked. "You were there for me when my friend got caught up. Not to mention the bomb ass orgasms you gave me." She blushed. Her soft hand caressed my cheek. "You hurt my feelings. Did you distance yourself because you are trying to make it work with your baby's mother? That was your family at the restaurant that night, right?"

"Fuck, no. Karen is my daughter's mother. I do not fuck with her. I met her there, so she could spend time with our daughter. I took her away from her a few months back.

That is the biggest reason I fell back. Plus, you have a man. I don't share, Val."

"I don't share either. So, before you try to pursue anything with me, you make sure your situation with your baby's momma is over. When the time is right, I would love to meet your daughter." She smiled.
"I ain't fucked with Karen in years. I want you, Val. I want you to leave that nigga." I was dead ass. Like I said, what I was feeling was crazy. It was foreign, but I fucked with the feeling tough.

When she stepped back and took a deep breath, I peeped the sadness on her face. It stung my heart. I knew she was about to diss me.
"Jam, the family is keeping it on the low. Tiger is on life support. They are asking us to make a decision. I found him unresponsive in the studio. He overdosed."
I wasn't expecting that. I rushed over and hugged her.
"Are you ok?"
"He is my son's father, and I feel bad for him. I even feel bad for his stanky feet ass momma."
I laughed.
"Sorry."
"Say how you feel, shit."

"I have a lot of love for Tiger. That is why I stayed. Plus, we have a son. I think I would have stayed just to keep my family together, but I have been tired." This time she pulled away, she stared into my eyes. I could tell she was searching for something, and I hoped I could help her find it.

"Am I a bad person if I feel like him overdosing was my only way out?"

"Not at all. Your feelings are genuine. As long as you own up to them, then you are being true to yourself. So, no, you are not a bad person."

Val pulled my face to hers, and our lips connected. I slid my tongue in her mouth and passionately kissed her. Never breaking our kiss, I scooped her up, and she wrapped her legs around my waist. Light moans escaped her mouth, letting me know that she wanted me just as much as I wanted her. Walking her over to my desk, I laid her on top of it.

The way she was looking at me with those dreamy eyes had my heart tight. This girl was heaven sent. My momma always told me that when it's real, it just happens. Real love will have you doing things you said you would never do.

"Make love to me." She pleaded. "Please."

As I was taking off my clothes, Val wasted no time taking off her one piece. With one quick motion, I was up on her and I buried my head in between her thighs. Her juices smelled as sweet as they tasted. The moaning and her pulling on my hair gave me ammunition to eat my bitch out like she was my last supper. Val didn't know it, but if she felt what I was feeling she would know that it was me and her until the end. I would express it to her, though.

After she came for me, I picked her back up. We kissed as I carried her to the wall. I slid into her and had to stop instantly to gain my composure. Baby's pussy was so tight and wet. She fit me perfectly. I knew I would have a hard time trying to hold my nut. I made love to her nice and slow until we both released.

"Am I crazy to say I think I love you?" The sincerity coupled with uncertainty in her tone, I knew at that moment that I had to be the confidence she needed to know that it's alright to love a nigga like me.

"We are both crazy then. I've been loving you."

We kissed.

"He better not send one picture of my baby to Aaliyah."

Tokyo

I didn't care what anyone had to say, I was happy. I had my family and my little girl. Dream was the prettiest baby in the world. I loved her because she was my own. Everything was going perfectly. I couldn't have asked for a better baby daddy. Dream was Jersey's heart and once Aaliyah got out of the way, he started showing me how he really felt about me. I knew it, but Aaliyah was in the way.

I thought after Aaliyah's ugly ass friend showed up acting ghetto at the baby shower, Aaliyah was going to be calling and writing to talk shit. However, to my surprise, I hadn't heard from her and that was best. I hadn't reached out to her since we talked about me getting custody of Dream. I felt it was best because I didn't want her to think that everything would be the same when she got out, nor did I want her to think that she could get any rights to my baby girl.

Dream was mine legally and just because we were sisters, we weren't making any deals. I told Jersey he better not send one picture of my baby to Aaliyah. He tried to argue with me about it, but I went the fuck off, and he left it alone. Dream was mine.

"Hey baby girl, wanna hang out with Momma today?" I cooed while picking her up.

I kissed all over her face. She was my everything.

Dream and I dressed alike. I dressed her in a Burberry romper. I had on Burberry leggings and a Burberry half top with a pair of red heels.

"Twins. Mommy and baby." I said, standing in the mirror. I snapped a selfie and sent it to Jersey along with a text telling him to put us on his IG. He hadn't posted me or the baby, and I didn't like that. However, that's another story.

I gathered all of our things and headed to the car. I couldn't wait to eat some good old barbeque. Momma lived almost twenty minutes away, Dream had fallen asleep.

We pulled up to my momma's house, and she was getting in her car.

"Where are you going?" I asked, switching the baby to my other arm.

"About to go get Mona and the kids." She shook her head. "Why? Where are they?" I asked. My stomach growled. I forgot I hadn't eaten, and the barbeque smelled good.

"Girl, she said Oscar found out the baby ain't his. Girl, she said when she got home, all her and the kids' clothes were on the lawn. He changed the locks on the door and

all that. She called me screaming and crying. The muthafucka was so cold, he was there waiting, calling her all types of dirty hoes. He took the keys to the car and told her to get the fuck off his property."
Dayum! I didn't know he was going to do all that. I almost thought the nigga didn't care. I sent that message months ago and he didn't say shit. I was over being mad with Mona and thought nothing else about it.
I kind of felt bad because she got the kids. I didn't think he would do all that. Yikes.
"Momma, watch the baby. I will go. I don't want you over there tripping."
She hesitated for a minute before taking the baby.
"If that muthafucka buck, y'all better knock him into next week. Fucking with my niece. I don't play about her."
"He don't want it." I retorted. "I'm going to take your truck. They all can't fit in my car." I told her.
"I'm not playing y'all lay that nigga out, if he acts like he want it. Old weak nigga. Going to do them kids like that."
"Right. He will get his, though."
As I backed out the driveway, I told Momma to change Dream and give her a bottle.

When I made it over to Carson, which was about fifteen minutes from my mother the entire neighborhood was out there being nosey. Mona lived in a nice two-story house. Well, not anymore. When I saw the police cars, I quickly parked and jumped out of the car. The nigga really threw all their shit out. That was fucked up.

I saw Mona holding her two-year-old, the one she got kicked out behind because she lied. All I could do was shake my head. She and a woman cop were talking. The other kids were standing next to her.

"Cousin, you ok?" I asked when I approached her.

She burst into a loud cry.

"I can't believe he did me like this. He claims our son isn't his."

"That's his baby and he knows it. Nigga did all this because he doesn't want to take care of his child, or he got a new hoe pumping his head up." I instigated.

I looked over at the cop car where he was talking to two officers. Oscar was fine as hell. He was bi-racial with soft curly hair and all that. He stared at Mona like he wanted to kill her. I wish his ass would've touched my cousin. He would've gotten beat the fuck up.

"The police said he just can't put us out like that. He has to evict us. I just wanna go. Help me get my stuff." She handed her oldest the baby boy.

I don't know why she wanted to leave. If they said she could stay, she should have stayed. She wasn't coming to my house. I was taking her straight to my momma's crib.

"I got you, cousin. He ain't gon' have no good luck."

The cops made Oscar help us get some of Mona and the kids' things. We loaded what we could. They ordered him to put the rest back inside the house.

"You know that's your son. Karma is a bitch." I said to him.

He held up a yellow envelope in the air.

"Nah, this is the proof. Now call my cousin and tell his broke ass to help you!" He yelled at Mona.

"Whatever, Oscar." Mona replied.

"Come on, cousin. He's just mad." I grabbed her by the arm. The kids were already getting in the truck.

"If I ever find out who sent me the message on IG, I am going to give them ten stacks. Glad I got you out my crib." Oscar taunted. I'm glad I wasn't hard for money because my cover would've been broken.

 Mona didn't even reply. She climbed in the truck and laid her head back on the seat. Tears ran down her face. It was sad.

"I bet it was Frankie's ass. He's mad because I won't fuck his broke ass no more.

When I see that nigga it's on." She threatened.
Frankie was the real daddy.
"I can have Jersey get Oscar." I instigated.
"He is going to get his too." Was all she said.
We got to my momma's house. I rolled my eyes at how my momma always tried to act as if Mona was innocent. That baby wasn't his, shit.

"You know what? Fifteen years from now, I'm going to be long gone from Cali. Me and my baby girl. If Aaliyah wants to live in the past, that's on her." I said to Macho. After taking a pull from the blunt, I passed it to him. I wasn't planning on living the rest of my life in Cali. I was going to make my money while I could and then bounce. Cali was overrated. Too many niggas hating.
"Naw. You know I got a fight coming up." He explained, using his hand to decline my offer to him hitting the weed.
"My bad. I forgot." I took another toke from the blunt. Weed was relaxing, but coke did the job. Took me to where I needed to be to not give a fuck about anything. I was glad I did a few lines before Macho pulled up.

Macho and I sat out by the pool talking about my little situation. He wanted to know how I felt about Val and her assumptions. Also, how I felt about how others may view Tokyo and I, raising me and Aaliyah's child together. It's like this, I felt bad about Aaliyah going down. I truly loved her. However, I didn't put the drugs in her car. Tokyo told me that she tried once before to take my drugs out of the house. This time she was planning to do something else with it. She should've left my shit alone.

Far as me fucking around with her sister, it was fucked up. Being around Tokyo as she helped me raise my child created a bond between the two of us and before either of us knew what was happening, we were a couple. That's my story, and I'm sticking to it.

"So you're going to get up and leave with the girl's baby before she comes home?" He asked. I shrugged my shoulders.

"That's the plan. Shit, that's fifteen years from now, who knows."

Like I said, I felt bad about Aaliyah going down, but it wasn't my fault. Tokyo had been on some real mature shit. Stepping up to raise her niece, my baby, and having my back. I appreciated that shit. After I paid Buddha back, I was broke. Tokyo looked out; she had faith in my hustle. I was eating with some heavy hitters now. And Frosty the dirty cop hadn't been popping up, so I could breath. I hoped he was dead.

Macho and I chopped it up for a little more before he stood to leave.

"I thought I was going to taste you before I left." Macho said, eyeing my crouch.

"Tokyo and the baby should be back soon. I'll call you later this week." I responded.

"Um, what the fuck is he doing here?" Tokyo questioned. I didn't even hear her ass walk up.

"Where is my baby?" I asked. With her eyes on Macho, she replied.
"She's in her room. Why is he here?"
"Man." I grumbled.

"Tokyo, it's like that? The three of us go way back." Macho teased. With a smirk on his face, he looked at me. "I'll be waiting for that call." With that, he walked out.

"Where are you going?" Tokyo snapped.

"To walk him to the car. Stop being extra." I cut my eyes and followed Macho.

After I came back inside, Tokyo went off. Suddenly, she wasn't feeling me and Macho's friendship. Typical bitch. I told her what she wanted to hear. I wasn't messing with the man like that anymore, and then fucked her into a coma. Tokyo was cool, but the bitch was crazy if she thought she was going to change me. I gave in for now, but trust me, wasn't no hoe going to run me.

"I was starting to feel like it was indeed a setup."

<u>Tokyo</u>

Three years later

Dressed in a Dior two-piece legging set and a pair of Tory Burch sandals, I climbed out of my G Wagon and walked into the salon. The smell of hairspray and R&B music greeted me at the receptionist's desk.

The establishment was immaculate, professional, warm and welcoming. It was an elegant hair salon and spa in the heart of Compton, California. I glanced around, checking the place out. The inside was spotless. Each styling station was clean and orderly. The bright sunshine streamed through the windows. The black and white interior design gave the salon a sleek and stylish look. There were large mirrors, fluorescent lighting, and red accents for a contemporary feel. The glossy red shelves and knobs on the wall shelf popped. Even though it was in the hood, I was impressed.

"Well, hello there. Welcome to Get Glammed By The Best. Do you have an appointment?" Asked the friendly receptionist.

Looking back at the receptionist, I replied. "I do. With Cali Girl."

"Ok." I watched as she looked at the computer and then back at me.

68

"Are you Miss Monroe?"
"Yes." I answered with a smile.
"This is your first time here?"
"Yes."
"Ok. For our first-time customers, we give a complimentary pedicure or manicure. Or you have the choice to choose a free thirty minute massage." As I was about to respond, a cute young black girl walked up holding a two-tier serving tray with fruit on the top and drinks at the bottom.
"I'll do the massage."
"Would you like an alcoholic beverage?" The young lady asked. "Or tea, water, fruit?"
"I'm fine, thank you."
"You're welcome." She said, walking away. The handsome massage therapist escorted me to a private room where I got a massage. He knew how to work with his hands. He was so good, had my pussy jumping. I couldn't help but wonder if he could fuck just as well. I wouldn't find out. My hoe days were over. I was a momma now. Plus, I loved my man.

"How did you like your massage?" The young lady who washed my hair asked.
"Girl, I loved it." I replied.
"He's good."
"Yes. I will book with him soon."
She giggled.

"If you think he's good you should try his twin brother. Girl, they both got hands."

"I'll keep that in mind."

"Ok. I'll sit you under the dryer. You'll be under for thirty-three minutes. Once we are done here, your stylist will be waiting. I'll be back."

"Thanks. I'll take a mimosa."

"Sure thing." She walked off and returned shortly with my cocktail. Thirty-three minutes later, I was sitting in my stylist's chair.

I was going through my emails. I had a client I was to meet after my appointment for a fitting, so I emailed her to reschedule. I missed my baby, and all I wanted to do was see her pretty face. Dream was my heart. I loved her with every breath in me, and no one in this world would ever change that or take her away from me. She was going on 3 years old and was so smart.

"Hi. Ms. Monroe?" I heard a sweet voice and smelled the scent of sweet perfume. I think she wore the fragrance HER by Burberry.

"Please call me Tokyo." I paused. Looking into the eyes of Cali Girl, who was Kash's sister that went to prison some years back, made my chest thump hard.

Lori referred me to her. She never said that was Kash's sister. That bitch knew what happened that day at his party. Why in the fuck would she set me up to get my hair done by a hoe whose brother disrespected me by posting what we did all over social media? My stomach cringed, thinking about how people saw me with his nut all over my face. I'd have the last laugh. I bet his jailbird ass wouldn't. No more football for you! Ha!

"Are you ok, did I say something wrong?" She asked. I quickly scanned over her outfit. She wore all white, but her feet were covered in gold YSL six-inch inch heels.
"Oh, no. You did nothing."
I sat there wondering if I should get up and leave. I was sure the bitch remembered my face. I decided to stay. I needed my hair done. If anything popped off, I would fight for mine but best believe I was going to sue the shit out of her.

"Oh my God. Now I know who you are." She said. I looked at her through the mirror. My dark skin turned red. I'm sure she could hear my heartbeat through my chest. "You're Tokyo Monroe, the fashion designer. Nice to meet you. You have an eye for fashion." She sounded sincere.

"Thank you."

The door chimed, indicating that someone came into the salon. I heard the receptionist's voice.

"Hey, Val. You're here for Boss Lady at 12, right?"

I turned and looked. I was distant, but I knew that hoe. Hadn't seen the bitch in person since my baby shower. Shortly after, she had been all over social media. She found Tiger, her man, dead. He overdosed. God doesn't like ugly. Seeing Kash's sister then Val, I was starting to feel like it was indeed a setup. I was so glad she was almost done. I was nervous, but I played it off.

"I'm going to get a Pedi." Val told the receptionist.

"I'll let you know when she's done." The receptionist said to Val.
Val didn't have to pass me, and I was glad of that.

"So, what are you doing for your brother?" Another stylist asked Cali Girl.
This shit was feeling more like a setup by the second.

I continued to browse through my phone, but I was all ears.

"We are throwing him a party on Saturday. Invite only. Check your email. Then Sunday morning the family's flying out to chill at a secret location."
Wait. So, Kash was getting out. I wondered how that happened. It's cool. Jersey had that shit on lock, anyway.
 I continued to pretend to look through my phone until she announced that she was finished. I looked in the mirror and when I say that bitch slayed my 36-inch curly weave with the lace frontal, she did that.

"Love it." I beamed with a smile, handing her five one hundred dollar bills.

"Thank you."

I got up to leave and Val walked up. Frowns crinkled her forehead. I gave her the once over. I wasn't scared of her. She was dressed in jeans and a tank top. It looked like she lost a little weight.

"Cali, I bet you didn't know you were fucking with a snake." Val announced.

"Girl, boo." I said, walking towards the door.

"Y'all, now she is playing house with her sister's baby and man. Her sister is in prison because of the nigga, and she's fucking him."

"Mind your business." I snapped back. I never stopped my stride.

"My best friend is my business."

"You should've died with your dope head ass man."

I walked out the door, ignoring the laughter and chit-chat. When the door dinged, I quickly looked back ready to fight.

"Get that camera off me." I demanded. It was one of the chicks in the salon. I turned around and was blinded sided. All I felt was a hard punch connect with my left eye. Gotdammit!

There is no greater blessing than a family hand that lifts you from a fall; But there is no lower curse than a family hand that strikes you when you are down.

"I swear, I am going to kill them both."
<u>Aaliyah</u>

Day 1,273 I sat in a woman's prison for something that was no fault of mine. Everything was looking up for me. I found out I was pregnant and planned to move to Atlanta, Georgia with my mother.

I didn't even get a chance to smile long before my world came crumbling down. I lost everything. My freedom. My child. And my mom. I would say that I lost Jersey, but he left me. No, he said fuck me. Jersey showed me the day he didn't care about me or our child when he never told the truth about those drugs being in my car. I couldn't understand how that stuff got in there. I didn't even see his scary scandalous ass at court. My mother told me he wasn't shit, but I was too far gone off the love I thought we shared to even see that what we had wasn't real.

Jersey broke my heart. It hurt me, and I was convinced that I would never love again. I just couldn't. A fifteen-year sentence behind a man and his bullshit. I felt so low, ashamed, and disgusted because I allowed love to screw me over. It hurt but nothing hurt more than giving birth to a baby who was taken out of my arms and away from me like it was nothing. I only got to see my baby girl for what seemed like a split second. Every time I thought about her and losing my mom, my rider, and my backbone, my heart crumbled. I suffered days at a time from it hurting so bad it felt like someone yanked my heart out of my chest, tossed it on the rocky pavement and stomped it with spiked heels right before running the muthafucka over with a big rig truck. My life changed within a matter of seconds. God. I lost all hope in him. What had I ever done to anyone to be going through some shit like that? My fucking momma was all I had, and she was gone. I wouldn't see my baby girl until she was 15. I hadn't even seen pictures of her. It had been three years since I saw her face. All I could remember was her smooth skin, jet-black curly hair, and almond- shaped eyes. I'm sure Jersey sent pictures by the weight of his letters. I never opened them. I couldn't bear to see her face when I wasn't even there to be a mother to her. I opened no mail. The last thing I opened was a legal document I received about signing my rights over to Tokyo. I never even opened Tokyo's letter she sent after she got the baby. I believed I would get around to them one day, but I still wasn't ready to hear from the outside world.

Laying back on my bunk with my eyes closed, I stared into the ceiling thinking about the next scene I would write in my new book. I wrote three books and wasn't sure if I would ever publish them. Writing, exercising, and doing the women's makeup had been helping me with my depression. I even taught my cellmate how to read at a 3rd-grade level. Writing and communicating with the women there was all I did. I wanted no parts of the outside world. I learned that to even try to heal, I had to act as if the people on the outside didn't exist.

"Hey, Monroe." Shannon, another inmate, called my name.
She was the prison's newspaper and even knew about what was going on outside of jail. She's the one who leaked I was the late Blair Monroe's daughter. Only a few knew who my father was. Everyone else was young and had no clue. It didn't get me any special treatment or anything. If anything, I gained the respect and support of others by simply being me. I was real, cool, inspiring, and low-key.

I opened my eyes and sat up in bed.

"What's up?" I replied to Shannon calling my name.

"I wanna show you something." She eased into my cell.

"Look at the video on social media. It's your bitch ass sister getting her ass beat." Shannon spat with much attitude.

I frowned up my eyebrows and turned up my lip. I never talked about any of my family on the outside. I was sure that they knew Tokyo was my sister, but no one ever mentioned family, let alone disrespected my family.

"Shannon, is there a problem?" I asked, looking her up and down. Bitches thought I was quiet, but after damn near killing a dike chick, they knew I could hold my own. I was the quiet, but angry one that they knew not to bother.

"Yup. If I get out before you, I swear I'm going to find that bitch and whoop her ass again. You good people, Aaliyah. I can tell. You inspire us here and look out for all of us. That's cold how she did you, but I'm going to handle that trick. You got my word."

Staring at Shannon, I was trying to figure out what she was talking about.

 With the shake of her head, she gave me a sympathetic look.

"Watch the video. I'll be back to get my phone." After saying that, she left out my cell. I stood there for a minute, trying to calm my racing heart. Something was telling me not to watch whatever was on the video, but my curiosity got the best of me.

Tokyo looked so pretty and even more mature as I watched her rise from the salon chair. Momentarily, I wondered who was watching my baby. I then saw my bestie, Val. She looked good too. She lost a few pounds, but it looked good on her. My eyes watered looking at the two of them, no matter the ups and downs my sister and I had. I still loved her, missed her, and most definitely appreciated her for taking care of my baby. Val, I knew she loved me. She was at every court date. When I was sentenced, it was her and my mother's voices that I heard scream and plead for my freedom. She had been writing to me too, but I hadn't responded to her either. God, I missed them. I missed being free.

I had to restart the video because I was so focused on looking at the two of them, I missed what was being said. I watched as Val had a frown on her face. She looked Tokyo up and down.

"Cali, I bet you didn't know you were fucking with a snake." Val said.

"Girl, boo." Tokyo replied walking to the door.

"Y'all, now she is playing house with her sister's baby and man. Her sister's in prison because of the nigga." Val announced.
It was at that moment my heart dropped. I blinked several times trying to figure out what was going on. Jersey and Tokyo were playing house with my baby. I could hardly believe what I had just heard.

"Mind your business." Tokyo tossed over her shoulder. She was ready to walk out of the door.

"My best friend is my business." Val snapped.

"You should've died with your dope head ass man!" Tokyo yelled, and then she walked out.

Another young woman had an iPhone in her hand videoing Tokyo and following her out of the salon.
"Get that camera off me." Tokyo snapped. Her focus was so busy on the chick that was filming, she didn't see the three chicks that were ready to attack her.

Bam! One girl's first punch hit Tokyo's eye and the other in her nose. Tokyo attempted to swing back, but she was too slow and outnumbered. I watched as she got stomped on camera by three girls. I could hear them name-calling and screaming out insults. The one who hit her with the first punch could be heard over the rest. "Nasty, bitch! I should kill yo' hoe ass!" She threatened.Tokyo collapsed to the ground and balled up in a fetal position. I watched in a daze as they stomped her ass out.

I was in total shock at the revelation. I didn't even know I was shaking while crying until Shannon came back.

"Don't cry, homegirl. I promise I will find her and beat that ass."

She slid the phone from my hand.

"I wanna watch it again." I told her. I watched it twice. I heard clear as day what was going on, but I wanted to see it one more time.

Shannon allowed me to look at the video one more time before she took her property.

"I swear, I am going to kill them both." I mumbled to myself. I meant every fucking word. That's if I didn't give up on life. I felt myself slipping into a deep depression.

"When I leave the game, I'll leave like a boss."
<u>Kash</u>

Clad in a pair of wheat Timberland boots, black designer jeans, a white polo T-shirt with a black P hat, I was looking G. I stepped out of my brand-new black on black Jaguar feeling like I was the muthafucking man. I scanned the parking lot entrance of the strip club called Crazy Girls. All eyes were on me. I loved that shit. I wasn't just a handsome, cocky nigga with swag, but a real ass nigga. That's why a lot of people showed me love. Like on tonight. My folks insisted on throwing me a welcome home party. I was with it. They rented out the entire club and did invite-only. I swear, it seemed like damn near the entire city came out. They may as well have let it be open to the public.

It felt good being home after being locked up in hell for three years. The pigs caught me slippin' once, but I bet it wouldn't happen again. I was arrested and sentenced to five years when I got caught making a transaction with a nigga from up north. Thanks to my lawyer for doing a good job with getting me the five years since they were considering giving me ten. Due to good behavior, I was out in three. To this day, I think I was set up but there was no proof. I was caught red-handed, so I had to take the deal. I lost my football scholarship and now the only choice I had was to take my throne in the dope game. I was a smart nigga. I bet I wouldn't get caught this time. Bet I would become the youngest nigga to do it. When I leave the game, I'll leave like a boss. I didn't plan on being in the game long, though.

Looking back at my homies, who had stepped out of their whips, I smiled. We all lined up in front of the club.

The four in the front were Yogi, Jam, Brandon, Chas and Quan. Between the homies and my sister, I didn't have shit to worry about. We were about to turn all the way up.

"I'm home." I cheesed.

"Hell, yeah!" The homies yelled.

"And, stay home." My sister added.

"Bet that." I replied.

The blunt was in rotation. Chas had a bottle of 1942 in her hand. We all chopped it up for a little bit before we moved towards the entrance of the club.

I mingled with a few outside the club before making my way inside. My crew was right behind me. Just as I was approaching the entrance, my eyes landed on a fine ass chick. I had to stop. I've seen some pretty women, but this woman was gorgeous.

"Why are you in line?" I asked. Giving her the once over, I took my bottom lip into my mouth.

None of the bitches I saw in line could hold a candle to Little Momma. She looked to be around 5'4, honey-coated complexion, with a body that was so muthafucking hot I didn't know if she paid for it or worked out. Little Momma was a little thinner than I liked but her toned legs, hips, ass, and pretty face made up for it. Just by her get-up, you could tell that she was one of those bougie chicks. She was dressed in a fitted baby pink two-piece tracksuit with high-top baby-pink colored Air Force 1 sneakers. She was blinged out in diamond studs, a tennis bracelet, and a sparkling diamond ring. The ring should have told me to keep walking, but it drew me to baby girl.

"Why are you standing in line?" I asked again because she and her friend acted like I was talking to myself.

"Because there is no VIP section and since my friend just had to come here, we are standing in line." She replied.

"Well, I am VIP." I told her. "Y'all with me. Let's roll." I put my hand out for her to take it. She looked from my open palm to my face and, of course, I flashed her my famous smile. At first, I thought she was going to have a nigga looking stupid but when she grabbed my hand, a nigga's chest was on swoll.

"So, are you with me?" Yogi said to her friend.

"Nah." Old girl replied. "I ain't bringing sand to the beach."

We all laughed. I felt her, though. I wasn't a nigga that brought my women out to socialize with me and my crew, but old girl who I had yet to learn her name had me stuck. I had some head that morning, but since I had been out, I hadn't had no pussy. I ain't the type of nigga that slang my dick around to any bitch. I ain't the type to double back, either. That's why I didn't bother to hit my ex, who had been calling since she found out I was out. I got head from the little side piece I was messing with before I left. It was something about old girl that had me wanting to be all up in her space. I wanted her to be the first piece of pussy I hit since being free. She was that bad.

"What you drinking?" I asked old girl. We were in VIP, chilling at one of the four tables reserved for me and my crew. Across from us was another table where my nigga Drako chilled with his crew. Drako was a well-known local rapper who old girl couldn't stop staring at.

I leaned in her ear.

"Drako got your attention, but you sitting over here with me. Should I be offended?" She peeled her eyes off him and looked at me.

"My bad. He's my ex-friend."

"The ex that put that ring on your finger or another ex?"

She looked down at her hand. Letting out an annoyed breath, she asked.

"Can I have a glass of wine?" I looked at the table and there wasn't any wine there. I flagged our waitress down and told her to bring over bottles of red, sweet, and bitter wine.

"Coming right up."

"Thanks." She replied. She reached up, grabbed my cup, and took my Patron to the head.

"I thought you wanted wine?"

She shrugged. I could tell that she was uneasy. More than likely, it was due to Drako being her ex-homeboy.

"I can make that nigga leave." I told her looking at Drako.

"Nah. It's ok. Let him watch me because I'm single."

"Me too. I'm Kash. I didn't get your name."

"I'm Rina and that's Joy." She pointed to her friend, who was raining cash down on a stripper. The waitress came over and brought the wine.

"I changed my mind. I want the good stuff."
She looked at the bottle I was pouring from.
"Say less." I made her a drink, added
pineapple juice and filled it with lots of ice.
I took mine to the head.
"I'm going to mingle with the homies. It's
my first time out since I got out of prison.
Enjoy yourself. But don't go too far." I
tossed her a stack of ones in her lap.
"Of course." She grinned. I stood there
staring at Rina.

Everything about her was sexy. Even the
way she tried to act like she was hip when
I could tell she was nerdy.
"By the way, welcome home." She smiled.
"Thanks, baby girl." I looked towards Drako,
and a stripper entertained him. That was
his best bet because the baby girl was
leaving with me. Fuck his homeboy.

"That bitch should've been scared to approach you had he had her in her place."
<u>Rina</u>

"So, you rolling with me?" Kash asked. His 6'2 frame hovered over me as I sat on the couch in VIP. Looking at him, I smiled. It wasn't just the drinks that had me giddy. Kash intrigued me. His handsome face and sexy smile had me ready to leave the club with him without even knowing him. Hoping my crazy ex didn't whoop my ass. However, that body of his would have a chick creaming in the panties just by touching his chiseled chest. I didn't give a damn about the consequences. Kash was easy on the eyes, and I was definitely digging his swagger.

I looked at Kash's hand, and he put it out for me to grab. Taking his hand in mine, he pulled me up. My head did a quick spin, and I could tell I was tipsy. That's why I liked wine. Once I sipped on hard liquor, I didn't know my limit. Which, normally led to me waking up the next morning with a banging headache feeling like a fool. But, that's another story.

"Let me tell my home girl I'm leaving." I told him.

Kash gave me a head nod. His white homeboy and a chick strolled up to him. She stood there while the white dude and Kash conversed. I walked away, wondering where I knew her from.

"I'm about to leave with Kash." I told Joy. She was talking to Kash's friend. Joy's eyes zoomed in on Kash.

"Isn't that the rapper Tiger's baby's momma next to him?" I looked back.

"Yes." I answered. "That's where I knew her from. Tiger was a rapper and died of an overdose a few years back. Rumor has it that, she wrote his music."

"She's got her a white boy now. I guess." Joy said. She then looked at me.

"Girl, if you leave with that man, you are going to get your ass in deep shit. I do not think that's a good idea. I also don't like the fact that O was sloppy to where a bitch was bold enough to send you those videos. That bitch should've been scared to approach you had he had her in her place, so do you. Just be prepared for the aftermath."

"First off, if he wasn't doing shit then he wouldn't have to keep no one in line. Secondly, there's no aftermath because I'm done with him. I hate him." I said angrily.

Joy bringing up what my so-called fiancé did to me had me hot. Every time I thought about how he gave another what was mine crushed me. The way he stroked her while looking into her eyes hurt my feelings. He didn't passionately make love to me.

It was only a video, but I could tell that tramp meant something to him. I was just a trophy that was kept on his arm for show and beat down when he was upset.

"I'm out. I'll send you my location." Joy and I hugged.

"I'm leaving in a bit, too. Love you and have fun, friend."

"Thanks."

I walked over to Kash. He wrapped his arm around my neck and pulled me in close.

"Alright." He said to his boy.

"Nice to officially meet you." He spoke to the chick I learned was Tiger's baby momma.

I waved at the both of them as I headed out of the club to be a bad girl with a very handsome bad boy.

I laid on the bed, using my elbows to hold the upper part of my body up. My kitty jumped. She was wet and purring, and I didn't know how much longer I could tame her hot ass. Kash stood in front of me, pulling on his blunt while butt naked. I swear, the man was perfect. Tattoos covered his toned chest and muscled arms. Across his stomach in block letters spelled out his name Ka$H, and underneath it was an AR-7. I liked it. He was daring anyone to play with his money. Old or young, it was something about a thug that turned me on. A square nigga could never catch my interest.

"You sexy ass fuck. That Pussy." He licked his lips while shaking his head.

I felt the same way about his long python that hung between his legs.

I was so drunk and would probably regret my hoe actions the next morning. At that moment, I wanted the stranger who went by the name of Kash to fuck my feelings away. I wanted Kash to give it to me so good I would forget about the heartache my fiancé caused. I knew he could do it. I had faith that his sexy ass wouldn't let me down.

 No longer able to wait for him to make me come, I took my two-fingers and rubbed them up and down my pussy.

"Mmm." I moaned, throwing my head back. I had mastered pleasing myself. It was unfortunate, but at least I got a nut.

Just when I was on the verge of coming, I felt Kash slap my hand out of the way.

"I got something better." His husky voice sent chills throughout my body. I opened my eyes and looked at him. His hooded eyes staring into mine.

"Mmm." I moaned when I felt his hardness touch my clit. For some reason, I knew this shit was about to be amazing. Kash rubbed his thickness up and down my pussy. He teased my center.

"Put it in." I begged, no longer able to take him teasing me. I was horny and in need of some hood dick.

"Give it to me, poppy." I moaned

"Say less." When he entered me, pleasure and pain took over. "Ohh." I cried out, scooting back. It felt like Kash ripped my pussy open. I wanted more, though.

"Don't run." He teased me. His strong hands pulled me by my thighs closer to him. When he entered me, I swear I was gone. Gone to a place that I hadn't been in years. Kash reminded me just how much I missed being dicked down by a nigga who took pride in pleasing a woman. The way he stroked me nice, slow, and hard switching his pace up at the right time had me climbing the walls.

"Fuuuuccckkkkk. This is sooo good."

"I'm about to nut. Come on you gotta nut with me." He growled.

"Okay. Okayyy!" I screamed. I could feel it. I was about to come again.

"Yeessssss." I was going crazy. I could feel him stiffen. I knew he was on the verge of releasing. I continued to work my hips.

"Fuck!" He growled, pulling out of me. I guess him pulling out was his way of being careful. We should've thought about that when we failed to use protection.

"That was so good." I admitted. "Do you think we can do this again?"
Kash chuckled.
"Hell, yeah."
By the time he came from the restroom, I was fully dressed.
"You think you can drop me off? I asked my friend to meet me back at the club."
He stared at me, making me feel uncomfortable.
"Nah. You can take an Uber back. I'll wait until it comes."
"Wow."
"No offense, but I don't know you. You could be trying to set a nigga up."
I couldn't get mad at that. I'd been around hustlers all of my life so I knew the rules.
"I'll wait in the lobby. You got my number." I said as I headed out of the room. Kash was right behind me. Once off the elevator, we went our separate ways. Watching him walk out the door, I wondered what type of man he was. Besides knowing how to fuck a girl senseless, I hoped he knew how to treat a woman. I wanted love and not be treated as property.

———————————

After I left Kash, I went straight home to my dad's crib. I was happy my father was out of town. Otherwise, he would have been here questioning the reason I wasn't home with my fiancé. I didn't feel like going through that with him. He believed that O could do no wrong. Every time I tried to explain to Dad how I was no longer happy being with O, he would blame it on our age difference and me needing to be more mature. I had never shared with my father how he would hit on me or how he was forever cheating. I was scared he would take O's side like he always did and that would crush me. I knew O was pissed. If he could drag me out, he would've but there was no way he could get on the premises. My father lived in an upscale-gated community. You couldn't come up unless your name was left with the guard, and the homeowner came down to escort you to their premises. I wasn't doing any of that. If my dad did, I wouldn't speak to him for a long time.

In a tank top and boy shorts, I eventually woke up and decided to go fix myself something to eat. It was five o'clock in the evening. Between the drinking and outstanding sex, I was burned out. I grabbed my cell so I could call Joy. I put the phone on speaker as her phone rang. I had the biggest smile on my face as I made my way down the circular stairs. I couldn't wait to share with my BFF how I finally got some good dick. I knew she would be happy for me.

Joy's phone went to voicemail.

"Bitch, call back. I wanna tell you about the guy from last night." I left on the voicemail.

I found myself thinking about Kash. I wanted to be his girl. I imagined him coming over sneaking kisses and trying to get a little pussy early in the morning while I prepared breakfast for us. I giggled at my fantasy, but wished it were true. The only time O showed affection was when he wanted pussy or when we were out in public, and he wanted to show everyone he had a young hottie on his arm.

It was crazy how me cheating back and enjoying it made me not even sulk at the video I saw of O and that ratchet hoe. Thanks to Kash and his penis, I wasn't feeling O no way. Nevertheless, after five years of being with the man, I was comfortable. Now stuck.

I ate the small breakfast I cooked and cleaned up behind myself. I decided I wanted to binge-watch Power. When I walked out of the kitchen, I stood there watching my father tongue kiss Patricia up. Patricia was Nita, my dad's girlfriend's best friend. They called themselves sisters. She had been to our gatherings with Nita a few times over the last two years. With that being said, I didn't know what the fuck was going on.

"Hey dad, and hey Nita's friend." I greeted sarcastically.
Immediately, they broke their kiss and glanced my way.
"It's Patricia. I know you're trying to be funny, but this is our business."
I raised an eyebrow. Before I could say anything, Dad spoke.
"Baby girl, what are you doing here?"
After giving the old scandalous hoe the death stare, I stared at my father.
"This is my house too, right?"
I then rolled my eyes and headed back up the stairs. Seeing my old man and his girl's best friend together disgusted me. People are grimy and only care for themselves.

"O just called me. He said he was on his way to get you." My dad announced when he stepped to the entrance of my room's doorway.
My head snapped towards him so fast.
"I'm not his property."
"That's your soon-to-be husband."
"No the hell it's not. Fuck him. It's over, and I don't care what you say." I jumped up from the bed I was sitting on. My dad walked into the room. Now standing at my bedroom door, I pointed out.

"What type of father are you? What type of man would continue to try to persuade a woman to be with a man she doesn't love. Is it because you work for him? Are you using me for that? My mother would–"
"Don't you bring up your mother. She left us, remember, so she's no better than me."
"She left because she was tired of your lies and cheating. If you had done right by her, she would still be alive today. You should've died, not her."

Wham! My dad backhanded me, causing me to damn near fall. I could taste blood from my lip. Then he grabbed me by the neck.
Initially, I was shocked when Dad gripped his gigantic hand around my throat and raised my entire body upward. My feet dangled. I couldn't breathe, but I refused to go out without a fight. I clawed at his grip, but he continued to choke me. My eyes rolled in the back of my head. A wave of fear surged through me. My father was trying to kill me. With every bit of strength inside of me, I upped my foot and kicked him right in the groin area as hard as I could.
"Fuck!" He bellowed. Releasing the grip, he had around my neck.
My body hit the floor with a loud thump. I held my neck, gasping for air. He bent over, falling to his knees.

"I'm sorry. I will never put my hands on you again. I'm sorry, Rina." His voice cracked with every word from the agonizing pain he felt. "I loved your mother. I still love your mother. I can't undo our past. I wish I could. I wish I could bring her back to you. I wanted you with O-"

"You're just like him. You're a cheater and an abuser, just like him. That's why you want me with him." I uttered. On my feet, I stood there staring at my father. Tears streamed down his face.

"Call an ambulance. I'm hurting so-"

"I ain't calling shit. You didn't no help when you had your big ass hand wrapped around my throat." I rubbed the side of my neck and continued. "You want me to be like my mom. I get it now. You don't love us." I ran across my room into the adjoined bathroom, slamming and locking the door. I screamed at the top of my lungs. I was more angry than hurt.

I swear I was done with my father.

"Life is a trip."

<u>Kash</u>

My mom and sister wanted to go out of town. I was really trying to get to work and make that paper, but I couldn't disappoint my girls. I loved my mom and sister with my whole heart, so even though I was on paperwork and wasn't supposed to go out of state without permission I was going. We were supposed to leave today to fly out to Vegas, but I wasn't going anywhere until my crew and I had our meeting.

Like I said, I was getting back in the game but this time full force. When I went to jail, I lost my football scholarship. The only thing I had left to do was make that shit happen like my daddy used to do before he fled.

"Alright, sister, run that shit back one more time." I said to Chas. We were in the house we called The Trap, talking business. Chas was like my right hand. Although I had the homies, I knew she wouldn't let shit happen to me. She told me that day not to do that play for my pops, but I didn't listen. I wanted to listen, but I had given him my word.

"Alright, so Yogi will be responsible for the city of Carson and Long Beach. Quan got Lancaster and Palmdale. I got the strip

clubs. Jam got gay clubs and colleges. Kash, you're responsible for making sure we got enough work to supply." She read off.
We all nodded. We sold powder, prescription pills, weed, and meth. I was done with the drops. We were taking over blocks... but this time none of us would get our hands dirty. We hired workers and the workers we hired wouldn't even know who hired them.
 I made sure we wouldn't be stepping on nobody's toes. The nigga O – was another heavy pusher. His spots were nowhere near where we would be doing business. If he had a problem, all I had to do was call my daddy. Mr. L.A. may have been out of the country, but he still could make shit happen.

We chopped it up about business a little more before the doorbell rang. Looking at the camera, I saw it was the pizza man. I was hungry as a hostage.
I looked down at my phone and saw I had a text message from Rina. Her pussy was good as fuck, but I could have kicked myself for hitting her raw. I was loaded and tripping. I didn't reply.

"Hey, Jam. Where is your girl?" I asked him. The nigga was in love. I could see it all over his face. She was cute, though.
"Can you call her? I wanna finish the conversation we were having about her

friend." Jam's girl Val was friends with Aaliyah Monroe, my former tutor and crush. I'd never forget the day they picked her up at the school. That shit fucked me up. Juicy was looking all scared. Learning that she went to jail behind that punk ass nigga Jersey had me hot. Val told me she got a lot of time. I told her I would get with her to talk more about it if she didn't mind. I felt bad for her. Both of us didn't get to finish school, something we both wanted. Life is a trip.

I thought about her and tried to figure out how I would be able to reach her to find out what happened. Shit, a week later I went to jail. I went to make a run for my pops, I had been putting off for months. I got tired of him asking and I went. Making the transaction, the police ran up and it was a wrap.

"She said she would be here in a minute. We about to take the kids out." Jam replied.
"That's what's up. You a family man, huh."
"Yup." He said with pride.
"That's what's up. I can tell you love her."
"The fuck out of her hot head ass. That girl crazy."
I laughed.
"Don't be talking about my friend." Chas said.

I text Rina back. She asked if we could hook up, and I told her I was leaving out of town. I made sure to let her know I would hit her when I got back.

Jam's girl came. She ran everything down to me, and that shit had me mad like it was me. Aaliyah was a nice lady. Fine too. Her bitch ass sister was cold. Jersey was just a lame. I found myself wanting to help her.

<u>Jersey</u>

I was sitting in the boss's office, sweating bullets. I didn't know what the meeting was about. The only time I saw 'Boss Man' was at our monthly meetings. So to be sitting in front of him as he laid back in his gold executive chair glaring at me, had me ready to shit my pants. To make matters worse he had niggas just as big as his 6'3 300lb ass standing on each side. They both held assault rifles with frowns on their faces.

"Don't tell me after all these years I got a bitch nigga working for me?" Big O spat.

I knew not to speak until I was given permission. I was scared, but still mad that he called me a bitch. I might have done some things the next nigga wouldn't approve of, but I was far from a bitch. I had heart. I may not have killed every nigga that got in my way, but I handled them my way. That shit counts.

My mind was going a mile a minute, trying to figure out what he knew. Did he know I liked getting head from men? Did he know I snitched on a few niggas? My brain was puzzled as to why the nigga called me a bitch.

"Speak." Big O ordered.

Big O resembled Rick Ross, but he was muscular and taller. I took my eyes off his lips and looked into his eyes.

"What problem do you feel I've caused, Boss?"

"J-Money." He called me by the nickname he gave me when I proved my work ethic to him. Right after Kash fired me, I met Big O. We had a family reunion and that's where I officially met him. I knew of Cuz based on him being in the music industry. He managed a lot of talent in the city. He was one of those producers that stayed in drama. He signed two local rappers that were bringing the noise. At the reunion, I watched how he and Uncle Warren interacted. I stepped to my uncle asking him how he knew dude and that's when I found out he's Cousin Rina's fiancé. Rina was beautiful and way younger than his old ass. She was with him for the money no doubt. I was glad I didn't skip the reunion as I did for the last fifteen years. I didn't care for my mom's side. They acted bougie. My dad told me how they cut her off when she was pregnant with me. Since my father blamed them for Momma's death, I did too. It never stopped me from getting invites to family functions.

"How in the fuck you let some niggas who ain't even from the hood come to town and start pushing work in our city? When L.A.

fled the country, so did his block days. You better put a stop to Kash before I end you."

Now I respected Big O. However, I wasn't with no one tossing around threats on my life. I'd get his operation shut down, niggas had to be careful who they tried to bully. When Tokyo told me she heard Kash was out, I wasn't tripping. Kash didn't run blocks, he did drops. I guess that changed.

"Speak." He growled.

"Me and my team on it. Trust me. I ain't about to let a nigga take food out my mouth. O, I respect you a lot. More than I do my uncle, but don't ever threaten my life." I stared at him, dead in his bloodshot red eyes.

He chuckled. When he was done, he looked at me with a serious expression.

"You handling this. You speaking up to a nigga like me. Good job. I've been watching you. You just earned a lot of points with me. Now get the fuck out and figure out how to take over all this shit."

"I bet your sister set you up."
<u>Aaliyah</u>

1year later

The sky opened up and a million raindrops tumbled down throughout the city. A gracious woman saw me exiting the bus without anything to prevent me from getting soaking wet. She offered an umbrella. She said that her daughter was picking her up, so she would use her jacket to cover her head. My heart was heavy, but I thanked her with a smile. I could feel the salty tears rolling down my face, and I tried to put my head down before she noticed.
"Is everything ok?" She asked.
I shook my head no.
"Well, it can't be that bad. You look healthy, and you are alive and free."
I'm sure the wristband from the prison and the brown paper bags were a dead giveaway of my situation. She was right. I was free. I still had eleven years left of my sentence, but here I was four years later out of prison. I should've been happy but how could I when everyone that meant something to me was gone or had betrayed me. Yes, I still had a little girl who I needed to be there for, but I had nothing. The courts wouldn't give her back. Not now, at least.

"Do you have a phone I can use?"
I watched as she went into her purse and handed me her phone. The lady reminded me of the singer Erykah Badu. The same pretty bronze complexion, beautiful chestnut-brown colored eyes, full lips and a welcoming smile. She looked to be in her early sixties, if that.

Mr. & Mrs. Hughes, my father's attorney, and his wife who represented me were the only numbers I still remembered. I stopped calling them after my mother died. Now that I was homeless and broke, I needed to reach out to them.

After learning of Tokyo and Jersey's betrayal, there was no way I was going back home. All I could think about was killing their asses. I couldn't do that and my daughter was there. No matter how alone I felt, I didn't want to jeopardize my freedom.

The phone rang several times before a man's voice answered.

"Mr. Hughes, it's me, Aaliyah."

"Aaliyah, good to hear from you. However, what are you doing on a phone? That can get you more time."

"I'm out of prison. I've been going back to court for the last six months. I'm free now. You didn't know?"

"No. I had no idea. My wife and I have been in the DR for the last year. We aren't coming back to the states. She hasn't practiced law in three years."

It took a minute to understand what he was saying. I wanted to ask what the hell happened, but it wasn't my business.

"Look, I'm using someone else's phone. I have nowhere to go. Are you still handling my father's affairs?

"We are not."

The phone became silent and when I looked at it, I noticed that he hung up. My heart dropped to the pit of my stomach. I stared into a daze. Something told me I was betrayed again.

I felt the lady ease her cell phone from my hand. Looking into her eyes, I saw empathy. I didn't want it.

"Thanks." I went to walk away, but she pulled me back towards her.

"My name is Ms. Myers. I ride the bus twice a month. It's part of my ministry. I travel by bus to see who it is that the Lord needs me to bless. Occasionally, it's prostitutes, drug dealers, single mothers. Whoever the Lord sends me to, I do not judge. I obey. It's not a coincidence that you and I crossed paths." She gave me a comforting smile.

Fresh tears ran down my face. My chest heaved up and down. I wondered what my next move would be. I felt so lost.

"I raised foster children for a long time. I have children of my own, but I knew there were other kids out there that needed my love. I've retired from that." She smiled. "But my kids still come to see me, and we have dinner every other Sunday and holidays. I help people. I will help you. Will you trust me?" She was so sincere. I truly believed this lady was an angel. I trusted that she wouldn't judge me from my past.

"I went to jail for something I didn't do. Drugs were in my car. They belonged to my ex. The same ex that is now raising my child with my sister as if she is her own. My mother died right after I gave birth. What it seems like is my attorney and his wife did something illegal and took all of my daddy's money, maybe my mom's too. Blair Monroe is my father." I blurted.
"The famous Blair Monroe? Whew, Chile." She giggled. "That man knew he could play a guitar and dance his behind off. Oh, and his voice." She fanned her hand.
"Thanks." I gave her a slight smile.
When she pulled me into her arms, I released a heart-wrenching cry. I hadn't cried that hard since the day I found out my mother passed away.
"What am I going to do? I don't deserve this."
"Baby, God makes no mistakes. Trust him." She advised. Rain poured down on the both

of us, but I didn't care, and she didn't either.

Bonk! Bonk! Bonkkk! A horn was very loud.

"Momma, what are you doing?" I heard someone yell out.

"That's my crazy daughter." She whispered. "Come on, baby, let's go."

I was reluctant to leave with her. One, I didn't want to seem like a burden. Two, I didn't know the lady or her family. However, for some reason, I felt like it would be OK, plus I had no choice.

She pulled away. Wiping my face with my shirt, I looked behind me. Ms. Myers was walking towards a black-on-black Maserati. Her daughter was in the driver's seat.

————————

"Joy Ann, she will be staying in the back house."

I watched as she shook her head. It seemed like she was used to her mother rescuing people. Once the doors automatically locked, Ms. Myers instructed me to pray and not worry.

"It never fails with you, Ma. At least I can say you haven't brought anyone to the house in a couple of years."

"I move when the Lord tells me to move. Baby, what is your name? I think I heard you say, Ali."

"It's Aaliyah"

"Wow, Mom. You don't even know her name."

"Hush up, Joy Ann. I have two bedrooms in the back of my house. It's normally for when family comes to town. Get you some rest tonight and tomorrow we will talk more."

"I have to see my probation officer in the morning."

"Probation officer. Oh, Lord." Joy griped, looking through the review mirror at me. She was throwing shade. I understood her reaction, though. I would have felt the same way had my mom brought a stranger to our home.

I didn't respond. Staring into a daze, I wondered how I was going to get ahead.

———

Ms. Myers had a nice home in the city of Torrance and from what she told me, she had more property that she and her grandson owned together. On the ride, I found out that she had three kids of her own. Joy Ann was 25 and the baby girl. The other two were sons. She had one grandson. She raised several foster children who still came around.

 The front house she lived in was a two-story home. I didn't go on the inside, but from the outside it was nice.

"What did you go to jail for, and why don't you have any family you can stay with?" Joy Ann inquired.

Ms. Myers had just shown me the back house she would let me stay in until the Lord told her otherwise. Those were her words. The inside of the small cozy house was decorated in white and gold. What I loved most was the picture window in the bedroom with the view of the mountains and her beautiful backyard. It was raining but the way Cali weather changed up, I was sure I might get to take a few swims in the pool before my time was up here.

"Joy Ann, she explained that to me already. You know I know she ain't lying, or she wouldn't be here."

"It's okay. You are her mother, and I would be the same way with my mother." I chimed in. I looked at Joy Ann who looked like a younger version of her mom. She was equally pretty and had a nice body. Her clothes were top notch. Looking at her reminded me that I had nothing but the clothing I went to jail in. All of my clothes were over at that house where Tokyo was staying with you know who.

"Come, and let's sit." Ms. Myers said. We took a seat on the gold sofa.

"I was framed." I started. Joy Ann's facial expression never changed. "It was the day after I found out I was pregnant. The day I was going to speak with my dean about me finishing my classes online. I was moving to Atlanta to be with my mom sooner than planned. We found out that she had stage 2 lung cancer and I wanted to be there with her." I could feel my eyes watering, but I refused to allow a tear to shed. I wanted no sympathy. "I pulled up to the college. I got out of the car. The next thing I knew I was surrounded by cops ordering me to put my hands up. I was thrown on the ground and arrested. All I remember him saying was, "You are under arrest for-" They popped the trunk on my car and showed me a very familiar bag.

"What do you mean?" Joy Ann questioned.

"It was my boyfriend's bag. It was the same bag that he kept in my closet. I knew what he did in the streets, but I always assumed he kept money in my house. One day, I curiously went into the bag. I was livid when I saw drugs. I snatched them up, ready to get them out of my home. My sister just so happened to see me and talked me out of confronting him. She said

I knew he was in the streets and as his woman I should have his back."

"How did the drugs get in your car? Did you put them there?" Joy asked.

"I had no idea they were there. I don't get it. He never drove my car. He said it was too girly and he didn't want people to know what kind of car his girl drove."

"So, what did he say when you went to jail?" Joy wanted to know.

"I haven't heard from him. He wrote to me after I was sentenced."

"You gotdamn lying." Joy Ann spat. She covered her mouth.

"Watch your mouth." Ms. Myers fussed.

"Sorry, Ma."

"Long story short, I had my baby in prison. My mother was in hospice at the time and died shortly after. I was forced to sign over my rights to my sister." I shook my head.

"Why aren't you staying with your sister?"

"When I was locked up, I found out that my sister and my ex were together."

"Together raising your baby?" Joy Ann inquired. She stood up from the seat and grabbed her key fob off the table.

"What's the address? I will go over there right now and snatch her up. Are you serious, Aaliyah?"

"Yes."

"Baby, you were set up." Ms. Myers stated.

I looked at her and no longer held back the tears. The more I thought about it, the more I believed I was framed.

"I bet your sister set you up. I bet you." Joy Ann countered.

"I hope you ain't lying." Joy said.

"I wish I was." I buried my face in my hands.

"How much time did they give you?" Ms. Myers asked.

"Fifteen years."

"You've been gone that long?" Joy Ann shouted.

"No, I only did four years. I thought my parents' lawyer was working it out. One day, someone came and said they were looking into my case. A couple of months later, I went to court. My sentenced was reduced and considered time served. I don't know what happened or anything."

"God is showing you that you are not alone."

We sat there for a few more minutes, talking. Ms. Myers said she was going to prepare dinner. She wanted me to come. I wanted to bathe and lay down. There was a lot on my mind. I had to figure out a plan. I didn't have no one at all. All I knew was I wanted my baby back.

"I'm going to run to Target and get you a few things. You look like you are about my size. There are snacks and stuff in the kitchen." Joy Ann told me.

I thought that was nice of her. Before I knew it, she walked up to me and hugged me.
"You will be okay. You gotta figure out a plan, don't give up.
Show them muthafuckas they can't break you."

———————————————————

"Yeah."
I heard Joy Ann say. I was in the room looking at myself in the full-length mirror. I hadn't worn real clothes in years. The stone washed Levi's, she got me was a size 13, and they fit perfectly. The Levi's were paired with a white fitted T that made me smile when I read it, 'Beauty. Brains. Strength. All in one.' A pair of ankle socks were covered by red low-top Converse. My hair had grown past my bra strap and my 190lb body was thick. Thank God, she got me edge control, so I could put it in a decent ponytail. I did not want to go around strangers looking crazy.
To be honest, I wasn't ready to mingle, but how could I tell a lady who welcomed me when I had nowhere to go.
 As I was finishing my final touch, I stopped when I heard Joy Ann talking.

"Rina? Where in the fuck have you been? Did he kidnap you, what the fuck happened to you? Oh my God, friend!" She yelled.

"Kansas. What? Why? Look. Are you in a safe place now? Okay, good. Momma is cooking tonight so I gotta be there, but I promise I will call you when dinner is over. Bitch, don't disappear on me either. I love you. Bye."

I walked out of the room and into the living room. Joy Ann was texting rapidly on her phone.

"Is everything ok?"

With her head still down in her phone, she replied.

"Girl, my best friend just resurfaced. She's been gone a year. Dipped off to Kansas. It's drama." She looked up at me.

"Okay, friend. You look nice, wait until we get you some real clothes and a real hairstyle. You are going to be killing these hoes."

"That's not my goal, but thanks."

"I know. My mom has always taught me to take care of myself. Looking good will make you feel good."

"I have so many clothes at the house. I kept myself up before this."

"And, you will keep yourself up after this."

"I am." That was all I said before walking to the door. I put my hand on my stomach. "I'm starving." It had been close to three hours since I arrived at the house. I showered, ate some fruit, and took a nap. I was now hungry enough to eat a horse.

"Let's go. I'll warn you. My nephew Buddha and I are the same age. My momma and his momma were pregnant at the same time. He and my brother don't get along, so at times they are tripping until my momma steps up. They know she doesn't play. Then I have a gay brother. He can be over the top, but he is cool. He's going to do your hair. He just doesn't know it yet."

I laughed. "Thanks for the warning. Thanks for everything."

"No problem. For the most part, dinners are cool. I look forward to it. On top of that, my momma can cook her ass off." She gave me a warm smile. "Don't look worried. Let's go." After that, we left out the back house and headed to the front. Several cars were in the driveway. I was nervous. I knew they would be thinking I was a charity case.

When I walked into the house, the aroma of soul food crept through the air. My stomach growled so loud. I secretly prayed that Ms. Myers was a good cook, like Joy claimed.

We walked into the dining room. There was a very long maple dining room table with twelve matching chairs. On top of it was a turkey, cornbread dressing, fried chicken, mashed potatoes and gravy, baked macaroni and cheese, a green bean casserole, candied yams, black-eyed peas, collard greens, and corn bread muffins. On a smaller individual dessert table was a pecan pie, sweet potato pie, and a triple layer chocolate cake.

"Let's go wash our hands." Joy suggested with excitement. "Then we can help finish setting the table." I followed her, admiring the nice house. My mouth watered thinking about the good food I was about to eat.

"Hey, nephew." I heard Joy Ann say.

"What's up, Auntie." The deep voice replied. I looked up and my heart dropped to my pussy. I was looking into the eyes of a very dangerous yet handsome man. Damn.

I couldn't believe it. Ms. Myers's grandson was the guy who Jersey owed the money to. The same guy who hit him with his gun when we were at the gas station. The guy who threatened me at the club.

He gave me the once over. With his bottom lip in his mouth, his eyes slowly scanned my body.

"I remember you." I whispered.

"So. Why are you here?"

"How do you know him? Don't talk to her like that. Momma is letting her stay in the back of the house."

He chuckled.

"My grandmother only takes charity cases."

"Fuck you." I snapped.

"Nah. You ain't my type. You like lames." He shook his head and walked off.

Suddenly I preferred not to eat, but my stomach thought differently.

"How do you know him?" Joy asked.

"Long story. But he's still the same as way back then."

I wasn't trying to put his business out there. I didn't feel right telling his family what he did to Jersey. It wasn't my place.

"I think he likes you." Joy teased.

"Well, I don't like him."

She giggled.

"I'm just saying. He's cool. Just mean, don't take what he said to heart. He's an ass, like you said."

"I agree."

"Let's go help Momma."

Buddha was on my mind. I knew I shouldn't have even been entertaining no man, but he had gotten even finer than the last time I saw him. From his smooth blemish free skin to his extremely toned body. His haircut was low with deep waves. He dressed like money and smelled almost as good as the food Ms. Myers cooked. Damn, that man had my panties wet. I should've been ashamed of myself.

Him calling me a charity case and being disrespectful should've been all the reasons I said the hell with him and ignored him, but at the dinner table, I found myself sneaking peeks of him. I was so glad he didn't notice. However, the smirk he would do every now and then had me wondering if he knew I was eyeing him.

 Joy was right her family was cool. It was just Ms Myers's biological kids there.

Last night was eventful, but a blessing. Meeting Ms. Myers and Joy Ann came at a perfect time. I would've probably been sleeping on a bus stop bench if I never ran into Ms. Myers. She was the sweetest lady and Joy Ann turned out to be cool. Of course, I wouldn't get too close. Females could be snakes, but I do appreciate her.

The food was amazing and running into Buddha... Well, that's another story.
Shaking my head just thinking how mean, rude, and fine he was. I was still shocked that I even ran into him again. Small world. "Momma, thank you for sending these people my way. It had to be you. Thank you so much. I know this is your way of telling me not to give up. That you are watching me. I don't know which way I am going, but I am sure you will guide me." I looked up and spoke to the heavens.
 Today was the day I would go see my probation officer. Ms. Myers offered to take me, but I chose to take an Uber thanks to Ms. Myers, of course. I didn't have a dime. I swear that sweet woman was God-sent. Being alone today would help me think some things over.
I tried to block out my thoughts, but to be honest, I was scared. Very scared. I was out here lonely. I didn't wish it on anyone.
 I text Ms. Myers from the prepaid flip phone that Joy gave me with her other items from Target, letting her know I was ready for my Uber.
Today I wore a pair of black Levi's and a white button-up shirt that belonged to Joy Ann. I still wore the same sneakers.
Ms. Myers told me the Uber was pulling up. I left out the door and when I got to the front, the Uber was waiting.

"I'm trying to figure out why you are still at my grandma's house." The deep voice inquired. I jumped. Turning around to see exactly whom I knew it to be.
Rolling my eyes at Buddha, I continued to the Uber.
Yeah, I wouldn't be here long. Hopefully, my PO could help me with housing.

____

I was in and out and, in my honest opinion, Ms. G wasn't any help. She questioned where I stayed and how I ended up there. I didn't have the address. So, I called Ms. Myers, and she gave Ms. G the address. I was taken aback when she wanted to talk to her. Ms. G walked out of the office with my phone to speak with Ms. Myers. When she came back, she handed me my phone.
"Here's a list of places you can seek housing. All the information they need is at the top. I suggest you stay where you are. Ms. Myers sounds like a nice person. I want you to take parenting classes and counseling. Also, you must get a job."
"I want to get my daughter back. Can you help me?"
"I'm not a family lawyer. Work on these matters first."
I gave her a head nod.
"I'll see you in a month."

When I left that place, my spirits weren't any higher than when I walked into the office.

I didn't have any money and didn't want to keep asking Ms. Myers to Uber me everywhere.

I stood outside, texting Ms. Myers letting her know I was ready for an Uber.

I looked ahead of me across the street and saw Bank of America. I could've dropped to my knees and cried. I completely forgot about the money I had in the bank.

"Thanks, Mom." I said, looking up. Today was going to be a good day, after all.

I didn't have an ID, but I knew for a fact they could pull my signature card to verify me.

I waited in line and when it was my turn, I walked to the counter. I had filled out a w/d slip for 5k. That would be enough for now. All I wanted to do was go shopping. Of course, offer Ms. Myers something. And hit the proper agencies to get my license and stuff. God is always on time.

"I don't have my ID. I'm sure my signature card is on file. I also have a passcode on my account."

"No problem. I'll pull your card." The teller replied.

Her eyebrow lifted. The way she was looking, I felt like something was wrong.

"Write your password on the back of this."
She asked, sliding me the withdrawal slip.
"Is everything ok?" I asked after she was
taking way too long to give me my money.
She looked around, shaking her head.
I watched as she wrote on a piece of paper.
"You don't have any money. Your accounts
were depleted."
"What? How? Why? Did they go dormant?"
I said in a panic. The teller had just told me
my accounts were closed. That couldn't be.
"How did that happen? No one had access
besides my mom and me."
"Let me get my manager." She walked away
and came back.
The manager came over to me and asked
me to follow her to her office, where she
would help me.
"Find the money, please." I said the moment
we sat down.
I watched as she typed on the computer. I
heard the printer go off. She got up grabbed
the papers from the printer and sat back at
her desk. After looking over what she
printed, she slid the papers to me.
"It shows your mother transferred funds to
her account. The CD you and her shared,
there was a cashier's check withdrawn
payable to herself and a Mr. Phillips."
"WHAT?"
I knew who he was; he was the man she
dated.

"Ok, my mom passed away. I'm the beneficiary of her accounts."
"Yes. You are. There's an account with 2520.67. I can withdraw that for you."
I forcefully wiped the tears from my eyes.
"Please, Ms. Thank you."
She gave me a sympathetic look before handing me a w/d slip to sign.
"I hope things work out for you. God bless you." She said as I left her office with more than what I entered in there with.

I didn't know what I did to deserve that. Everyone betrayed me. It was at that moment that I could feel my heart turn cold. I wanted revenge. No passes.
Ms. Myers: Baby, are you ok?
Me: I missed the Uber. I will be there later. I just need some time alone.
Ms. Myers: Can I send you an Uber to take you somewhere?
Me: No, thank you. I will see you later.
Ms. Myers: Be safe.
Me: I will.
With a heavy heart and a disturbed soul, I walked until I stumbled upon The Yard house.

"All I needed was someone to notice me."
<u>Rina</u>

"Now, why in the world did you just up and leave?"
Joy Ann asked.

"Besides wanting to get away from O and having no support from my father, I wanted out, and I knew if I went there no one would find me. Plus, I would have fewer chances of my secret being revealed."

Not giving her a chance to respond, I climbed out of her truck headed to the entrance of the restaurant. The warm weather felt beautiful against my skin. I took a minute to look at all the nice buildings. It felt good to be back home. I wasn't certain if I would be back permanently. It depended on how things went.

"Don't rush off." She called behind me.

I laughed. I wasn't rushing off, I just didn't want to talk about it until we sat down. I knew for a fact when I told her what I believed to be my biggest secret, she was going to flip.

The restaurant had been upgraded and looked nice.
We were seated in less than five minutes. I ordered my favorite fried broccoli and crab cakes. Joy ordered a salmon salad and four lemon drop martinis.

"It's something different about you, Ri. What's up?"

"Should I start from the beginning?"

"I think that would be best. Why leave out anything, friend?"

I knew she was being sarcastic. She was my friend, but I had to keep her out of the drama. She was safe that way. O was powerful and she would be the first person they contacted.

Over the music, laughter and loud talking could be heard. I hurried up, put my shades over my eyes, and pulled my baseball cap down. From their voices, I knew I heard men. I didn't want anyone noticing me.

"What's going on?"
"Has O or my dad ever reached out to you?"
"Nope."
Then it hit me. They probably were watching her and when they could never

trace her to me, they knew I wasn't with her.

I was about to start, I just wanted to get it over with, sharing my troubles with someone besides my great aunt who I stayed with in Kansas.

After the waitress set the drink down, I took two nice sips. I watched as the loud group was seated. From what I could see, I didn't notice any of the guys and that was a relief. All I needed was someone to notice me and run to O.
I took another sip from my drink and stated.

"O had been beating on me and cheating. If he got mad at something that was going on outside of our home, he would abuse me. Never in my face or leave visible marks. If he wasn't raping me, he would use belts and stuff. He blamed his reason on my mouth and always claimed I was flirting with his friends. I didn't want to tell my dad because he always took up for him when I complained. I was scared he would sweep him, hitting me under the rug. And, it would've broken my heart. The day I saw the video, he had just beat me the night prior because his homeboy told him that he better not fuck up and lose me. He told him

I was a diamond in the rough. He blamed what another man said on me."
" I got tired. I wasn't happy sexually, either. Mentally I was fucked up, but deep down I knew I deserved better. The night I left, I slept with Kash."
My heart fluttered thinking about him.
"My dad wanted to know why I was there and when I told him, he didn't have my back. I told him he was the reason my mom died. He slapped me. Then he tried to choke me out."

"Slow down." Joy put her hand up. "This is too much. I don't know if I wanna cry or go beat both of their asses. Oh my God, friend." She took the napkin and wiped her face.

"There's more."
She shook her head.

The waitress set our food on the table. We didn't even touch it.

"I kicked my dad right in between the legs when he had me in the air choking the life out of me. He fell down to his knees. I went to the room and laid down after that. When I woke up, O was standing over me. My dad snitched and told him I was there."

"What type of shit is that?"

"That day I knew I was done. Done with them both. O ordered me to come home. While I gathered my bags and talked to my dad, I called 9-1-1. I shocked the shit out of them. I told the police I was scared for my life and asked if they could escort me to a women's shelter. O and Daddy looked like they wanted to kill me. Once I was in the car, I had them take me to the airport. They waited with me. I got on a flight to Kansas. I left my cell phone behind."
Joy stood up.
"Give me a hug."
"Not here, I don't want to make a scene."
"Girl, I wish a muthafucka would. I got nine rounds for their asses."
"Joy, I gave birth to a little boy out there." I blurted.
"What?"
"He's two months. At first, I didn't know if he was by O or Kash. That baby looks just like Kash. I came back to tell him and hopefully get my life back."
"I can't believe this." She put her hand on her forehead.

"Calm down, girl, we do not fuck with people like him."

<u>Aaliyah</u>

I sat at the yard house for over two hours. I picked at the steak and mashed potatoes I ordered, but the four drinks had me lit. I didn't even have to standup to know that I was buzzing. Although, when I tried, I failed terribly.

While I drank, I blocked out all the bullshit that happened in my life. I just wanted to numb the pain.

"Excuse me." I flagged the waitress down.

"I don't think you need another drink." She smiled.

"Why, do I look drunk?"

"No, but when you went to stand up, I saw you fall back down. Is there someone I can call?" She asked.

"Not really. If you can get me an Uber, I will pay you."

"It's on us. Give me the address, and I'll have my manager get you an Uber."

I gave her Ms. Myers address and thanked her. I'm not sure how long later, but she told me my Uber was outside and was even willing to walk me.

I was drunk, but just like in jail when we made Puno I was the one who could control my liquor. I hated to seem like I had no control. Which in reality I didn't. I was homeless, barely had money, and lost my child. I didn't have shit under control. However, I believed I could walk to the Uber with no help.

"Damn, you're always bumping into people."
I was now familiar with his deep voice.
I looked into his handsome face and frowned; the way he acted made him look so ugly. With his good smelling ass.

Calm down, girl, we do not fuck with people like him. I told my jumping kitty.

"What the fuck? You always gotta be so rude?" I barked.

He looked at the waitress.
"I got it from here. Thanks for calling."
"What?"
I ice grilled the waitress.
"I recognized the address. My niece stayed with Ms. Myers before she passed. I remembered the address, so I called her." She explained.
"Did I ask you to call her? If I wanted to call her, I would've done it myself."
"Man, shut up. She ain't no shady bitch or sneaky. She did right."
Buddha grabbed me by the arm. I snatched away, damn near breaking my shit.

"Are you throwing subs?" I looked up at him, frown on heavy.

"Ain't got to. What, you got a problem?" He walked up to my face. His chest touched my breasts. When I say I was getting hot, that's an understatement. My kitty purred. I could feel her leaking. I was torn between slapping him and wrapping my arms around his neck and kissing on his sexy pink, full lips.

"Stop staring. Girls like you-" He cut it off in midsentence. "Never mind, let's go."

I wanted to put up a fight, but I knew his mean ass would've put up a better one. Reluctantly, I allowed him to grab my arm and walk me out of the restaurant like I was some child.

It surprised me that Buddha had manners. He opened my car door and even buckled my seat belt.

"Thanks." I said when he finished.

"Don't feel special." He shut my door.

Ignoring him, my body melted onto his peanut butter leather seats. I laid my head back and closed my eyes.

I heard him climb into the car. I could feel him looking at me, but I ignored him.

"'Man, don't throw up in my car."

"I can handle my liquor."

"You better."

Buddha turned on the music. The R&B artist The Weekend boomed from the speakers.

I let the window down. I knew he probably thought I needed to sober up. The air felt good.

"I'm not drunk, you know." I informed him over the music.

He looked from the road at me. I caught the annoyance on his face. Buddha looked back at the road.

I couldn't stand him. So damn rude. He had a loving grandma and family but walking around just nasty. People took life for granted. It's not until they experience living in this world alone that they realize just how lucky they are.

The second we pulled into Ms. Myers driveway, I took off my seatbelt. I couldn't wait to get the hell away from him.

"I know one thing, you better not bring no shit to my grandma. I don't know if you are on the run because your wack ass nigga tried to play somebody else. I don't play about my family."

I chuckled. Looking straight ahead, I bit my bottom lip. I was trying hard to keep my composure. After all, I was at his family's house. I didn't want to disrespect Ms. Myers like that.

"I'm sure you know why I'm here."
"My family don't run their mouths. My granny normally has a good judgement of character, but it's something about you."

I jerked my head towards him.
I couldn't hold it anymore.

"Listen. You don't know a fuckin' thing about me."
"I know you threatened to call the police on me because your lame ass nigga was going to get killed if he didn't pay me those sixty stacks."

"Sixty?" I said, more to myself. Jersey told me he owed mean ass 100k. I was going to give him that to pay him.

"I know I saw that nigga all on IG with a celebrity ass baby shower with some chocolate fine bitch. Shit, it wasn't long after you was trying to play captain save a lame. So let me guess. You found out he got somebody pregnant, and you left him only to have nowhere to go."

My leg shook. Something it did when I was angry and struggling to calm myself down. I could feel the hot tears running down my face. I was pissed and angry with myself because I was crying. Not because of stupid assumptions, but because it hurt. Being betrayed by someone that I loved hurt so bad.

"Don't assume shit. It makes you sound like a dumb ass." I climbed out of the car. Holding the door open, I leaned inside. His face held a scowl as he glared at me.

"The girl you saw Jersey with is my sister. My sister and my ex are raising my little girl." My lip trembled. I could feel fresh tears falling. My chest heaved up and down. "They are raising my little girl because I went to prison for drugs I didn't even know were in my car. Drugs that I'm sure belonged to my lame-ass boyfriend. A person who claimed he loved me but let me do time for something that had nothing to do with me. So, now two people who betrayed me are raising my daughter. Oh, and I'm here because my mother died while I was in jail. The majority of the money I had in the bank is gone. My father's lawyer fled the country, so I have no access to my inheritance. That's why I'm here. I would never bring harm to no one who helps me. I'll never betray a soul. So, why did this happen to me?" I boohooed. "You walk around here being mean to people, and you don't know the shit they've been through."

Fire filled my eyes. I stormed off, slamming the door so hard the world shook. Asshole!

<u>Buddha</u>

I wasn't even going to come here and say shit because I ain't want to fuck with y'all like that. I know y'all fuck with Aaliyah and y'all ain't about to be talking shit about a nigga when y'all don't even know the real.

I'm a real ass nigga, and I'm going to keep it G. The first day I saw her, and she talked that shit about calling the police after I popped that lame-ass nigga Jersey in the head with my pistol, I wanted to yoke her ass up. I didn't hit females, but I wanted to pop her in the mouth. Everybody from the hood knows you don't threaten to call the punk-ass police on a hood nigga. The only thing that stopped me from hitting her was me feeling like my grandma's psychic or prophet ass would find out. Plus, she was cute. Thick and sexy.

When I got out of jail and went to look for Jersey, I had already done my research and found out what I needed to know, so I could do what I had to do. I didn't know he was going to be at the gas station that day, but I was in the neighborhood when I just rolled past his girl's house. I ain't no creep ass nigga or nothing, but I had pictures of old girl. I took them, so I could show the nigga that I wasn't playing. I was coming for everyone. I wanted my money.

The night I saw her at the club, she looked so damn good I wanted to step to her on some 'Leave that old lame ass nigga and get with a real nigga like me' type shit. She was scared of me, I could tell. I could also tell that she was feeling my handsome ass. I saw it in her eyes. She better be glad she scurried off that night, or I would've probably got up in her- in a good way.

I thought about her a lot, and the shit was weird as fuck to me. Now I know what muthafuckas mean when they are like, 'It's just something about her.' It is, though.

When I saw her at my grandma's house, I didn't want to admit it, but I felt it was fate. Aaliyah was supposed to be my girl. I was giving her a hard time because I didn't know how to express myself. Plus, I was mad that she got herself in a situation like that.

I am going to be man enough and say I should've apologized last night, but I didn't do it. I would today.

I was donned in a gray and red Tupac T-shirt, a pair of black designer jeans, my black BB Simmons belt, and the red and black 1's. I'm a flashy nigga, so you already know, five chains, and two Cuban bracelets to match my Cartier watch. I had diamonds

in each of my ears and a small one in my nose. I needed to get my plaits redone, so I wore a black L. A. hat to cover the fresh growth.
I called my driver before I got dressed.

"What's up, Boss." My driver spoke.
"Sup, Diego." I spoke to my driver. I climbed into the black 2020 Cadillac Escalade. He shut the door. I picked up my burner phone and hit up my people. It was payday, and we were about to slide to a few hitting spots. Then I was going to hit my granny's house. I had to finish the backyard. I don't know why she ain't hired nobody to do it. Talking about, I needed to do man stuff and helping around the yard is what men did. I wouldn't dare tell her no.

In six hours, I made 10k. After dropping everyone back to their cars, I told Diego to take me to my grandma's. I was looking forward to seeing Aaliyah.

<u>Aaliyah</u>

When I woke up the sun was shining bright. I turned Pandora on the Mary Mary gospel station as I was getting dressed to start my day. I was in my feelings about how Buddha pissed me off, but I cried, prayed, and cried some more. When I woke up, I felt better. As long as I was here at his grandma's house, I would just avoid him. It was best because I swear the next time he comes at me sideways, I may just be finding another place sooner than I planned. I was going to go crazy on his ass.

I headed to the DMV, then the LA county office to get a copy of my birth certificate, and the social security office to get my social security card. All of the important documents I needed to get a job and even register for school. Last night I promised my mom and myself I was going to move forward. It hurt being out here with no one but as Ms. Myers said, "I'm free and each day I wake up is another chance I have." Deep down I didn't feel that I was going to get my daughter back, but I would try until my last breath.

I was then going to the mall to grab a few items.

I left the house at eight o' clock that morning and was finished with everything by three o' clock. Hungry and tired was an understatement. Joy texted me, asking where I was.

Me: leaving the mall
Joy: wanna hang out later?
I thought about it for a minute. Sitting in the house was depressing. On the flip,
I felt guilty about having fun when I didn't even have my shit in order.
Me: I'll pass.
Joy: you can't sit in the house; all you do is think about the past. It's time to move forward. It won't hurt you to enjoy yourself.
Me: ok, I'll come.
Joy: good. I will be there by 7. My uncle is going to do your hair. TTYL
Joy: K. Thanks.

I decided to go back inside the mall to find myself something cute to wear. I wasn't trying to spend a lot, so I hit H&M. I found this one-piece black sheer jumpsuit. I went into Aldo's and bought myself a pair of black stilettos. I then made a stop at the nail salon and got pampered.

I was at the counter paying the clerk when I felt someone staring. I looked up and it was Mona, Tokyo's cousin.

She looked different. She was dressed in a white V-neck blouse, black-colored tight high-waisted jeans, and some cute black and white wedge heels. Her super-long black braids hung down to her butt. Mona was what you would call a hood chick who swore she was classy. Loud red or blonde hair, she wore anything tight, and her nails were always long enough to touch the sky. She changed a lot. I guess time will do that.

"Do you have a number on Tokyo?" I asked.

"I don't fuck with Tokyo like that. Her mouth is unfiltered, have you ready to bust her in her dicksuckers. I ain't got time for all that. I think she got a new phone." She shrugged. "I been stopped fucking with her." I watched as she scrolled through her phone. "She kicks it with the same females she was talking shit about for years now she acts like she is Kim Kardashian or somebody. Happy that they are her friends. She's such a narcissist. Them bitches saw me and looked at me like I got shit on me. She done told them some lies. Hoes don't know me and I don't know them, it's all Tokyo! They better be glad I'm changing. She fooled me for years, the real her came out more." She looked at me. "She did you wrong. She violated. She is such a good actor, the bitch is good one day you'll look up and her evil ass will have a knife in your back. I'm sorry she did you like that."

I didn't respond to anything she said. I remembered she used to act like Tokyo could do no wrong. Like Tokyo was the best cousin in the world. She was always taking up for her, but now she wanted to talk about her. I didn't trust people like that. At the end of the day Mona was cool people but I'm cool on anyone that has dealings with Tokyo. She's toxic."

Mona read off the number she had on her. I thanked her. I prayed it worked.
"Don't worry. Every dog will have their day." She said.
"Thanks for the number." I hurled over my shoulder.

I started to call Tokyo, but I thought about it. She was a snake. I wanted to surprise her.
I pulled up at the house.

There was only a black Jeep Wrangler in the driveway. The driveway gate was open. With every step, my heartbeat quickened. Today was going to be the day I saw my baby again. I was going to try to prevent it as much as I could, but if Tokyo said anything stupid, I was going to break her muthafucking jaw. I prayed Jersey wasn't there.

I rang the doorbell to my own damn house. Looking around, much hadn't changed. The flowerpots on the porch took me by surprise because neither of us had a green thumb. I heard a key enter the doorknob, when the door opened the smell of pine hit my nose, which surprised me. Tokyo never liked cleaning and felt comfortable living in a pigsty. I was the neat freak that constantly cleaned up behind her. Tokyo was so nasty I wouldn't have been surprised if I saw roaches in there riding around on motorcycles. By her appearance you wouldn't think she was so lazy and nasty.

"How can I help you?" The person asked. It was a middle-aged white woman.
"Hey, I'm Ms. Monroe. I'm Tokyo's sister. I am also the other homeowner." I replied.
"Oh, ok. How can I help you?"
She stood there with a raised eyebrow as if she was confused.

"May I ask who you are?"

"My name is Miss Grace. I'm the tenant. I've been renting this place for almost two years."

I blinked rapidly. The bitch Tokyo had the nerve to rent out my house.

"Oh, really?"

"You should've known this, right? You're the other owner. Oh, did she not tell you?"

"No, she didn't. I do apologize, but you won't be here for long. Start searching for a new place to stay."
I stormed off the porch. I wasn't mad at her. I was angry at Tokyo. I wasn't playing so I said the tenant had to go.

It upset me. I cried once I got in the Uber. I wanted to pull to Patricia's house hoping Tokyo would be there, but something told me to go home.

"The nerve of that bitch." I spat. I flopped down on the bed. I was a lot calmer than I was on the ride back home, but I was still in my feelings.
I didn't even go get anything to eat, I came straight to the house. All I wanted to do was hop in the bed and cover my head, hoping to wake up and all this will be a dream.
Once I got in the house, I said fuck that. The house being rented by shady ass Tokyo

wasn't the end. Legally, it was my house too, and I promised myself that I would benefit off what was mine. I had a trick for that girl, and she didn't even know.

It was still nice and warm outside for it to be after four o' clock. Ms. Myers called to tell me she had a few errands to run. No one was there but me. I prayed Buddha didn't show up. The way I was feeling, he better had stayed far as fuck from me. Talking that mess last night. I could've slapped him.

Looking at the clock on the cable box, I still had over three hours before Joy showed up. I was now anxious to go out. I recognized the devil wanted to steal my joy, and I wasn't about to let that happen. I was still hungry, so I ordered pizza. At the mall, I picked up a cute little two-piece bathing suit because I had been dying to get in the pool. Before going to jail, I would have never, but I lost that pudge I once tried to hide while in jail. Not bragging, but my body was right. I looked hella good. I was the real definition of slim thick. Those jail workouts were the business.

I took a quick shower, I put baby oil on my body and a little suntan lotion plus sunscreen. I slid on my orange two-piece. I did not know my booty was that fat. I turned from side to side, admiring my nice round plump ass. I snapped a picture of me on my cheap prepaid phone. Ponytail and no makeup, I was still cute.

 In the kitchen was wine. I poured myself a glass and sat on the counter. I ate a banana until the pizza arrived.

Standing near the pool, I sipped on my glass of wine. I thought about when my dad and mom would sit by the pool and watch me swim. Daddy used to call me a mermaid. That's when he wasn't on the road. I loved when he spent time with me. I always loved water. It was one of the most relaxing tranquilities.

I sat the glass down and dived in the pool. I could swim like a fish, so it took me no time to do two laps. I forgot about all my problems as I floated on my back. I did a few flips in the deep end and when I came back up, I took a deep breath and let it out.

"My pizza." I said, opening my eyes as I emerged from under the water. Remembering, I was hungry and had ordered food. Swimming back over to the wall, I grabbed my phone to see if there were any missed calls from the pizza delivery person. Climbing out of the pool, I remembered I didn't have a towel. I hurried into the house.

"What the fuck?" I snapped. Buddha came walking out the door, eating a slice of my damn pizza. I wanted to knock it out of his hand. The nerve of that hungry bastard.

"If looks could kill, I would've been dead."

<u>Buddha</u>

"Man, you ain't going to no club tonight, always trying to be around some hood niggas." I said to Aunt Joy. We were on the phone. I stood in my granny's front yard. I'm older than her by one year. So I get to tell her what to do.

When I pulled up and didn't see my grandma's car, I called the old lady, but she didn't pick up, so I called Joy to see where she was and that is when she asked me if I was going to Quan's birthday bash.

"I ain't listening to you. Me and the gang going." She sassed.

"Who is your gang?" I wanted to know. My eyes narrowed in on a black car pulling up, I went for my waist. Me being a young nigga out there, a young nigga that got major bread with the snap of a finger... niggas be hating. Especially when I go on one of my splurging sprees. Call me a bragger, but I love to be on IG flashing thousands or doing videos when I go purchase a pair of shoes that cost as much as a nigga pay his momma to live with her. Niggas wanna say I ain't getting my shit out the mud, why because I ain't go kill a nigga and his family to get what I wanted. I ain't with that, but fuck with my paper and your ass will have my choppa down your throat. Niggas knew not to fuck with me. I didn't broadcast my business, but I had a few properties that I owned with my granny and a daycare center.Our businesses assisted low-income parents. People didn't see the good I did, and I didn't give a fuck, but my flashy lifestyle made me a target for the haters.

"Me, Rina, and Aaliyah going." She named her gang.

I watched as the Mexican dude got out of the car. Just because he had a pizza box in his hand didn't mean shit.

"Pizza for Aaliyah Monroe."

I gave him a head nod. Removing my hand from my waist, I took the pizza box from dude's hand. He must've seen my heat on my waistline, he got the fuck on. I was trying to give his dumb ass a tip.

"Rina? Where she come from?" I asked, I ain't heard her name in a minute.

"It's a long story and if she wants you to know, she will tell you but back up because she got enough shit going on."

"I don't want that girl." I retored.

I headed to the back of the house with Aaliyah's pizza.

"I know you don't want her because you want Aaliyah. I saw how you were-" I hung up in her face. Leave it to Joy to call a nigga on his shit.

The door was open, so I walked straight in. I placed the pizza on the counter. I called her name a few times, and she didn't respond. I just so happened to look towards the living room window and saw her in the pool. She was floating on her back. Her titties looked good peeking from under the water.

"Calm down, boy." I said to my dick. I watched and could tell that she was in a peaceful state. I thought about how that nigga Jersey fucked over her and I wanted to protect her. Show her what it's like to be loved and adored by a real nigga. Just like that, I got pissed off. Joy was trying to have her at the club. Kash and his crew would be there. I remember the day me and that nigga Kash got into it in his momma's backyard over her. Nigga was mad when I said I pressed her about the shit me and Jersey had going.

Joy was crazy if she thought Aaliyah was going to the club with her, that nigga would never get that one. I already deemed her mine.

Finally, she came up from the water and eventually climbed out of the pool. I grabbed a slice of pizza and headed out the door, bumping right into her.

"What the fuck." She snapped. "Why the fuck are you in my space eating my damn food?"
I didn't respond. I only stared at her. I knew she was pissed with me, and I had to figure out how to apologize. I wasn't used to that. She curled her lip up as she stared at me. If looks could kill, I would've been dead.
"So you just going to stand there looking stupid."
I was trying hard as fuck to keep my eyes trained on hers. I knew once I took a good look at her sexy body, I was going to do some shit that would result in her slapping me or me fucking her brains out.
"I'm sorry about last night. You're right, I should have never assumed. I apologize, you are going through enough." I was sincere as fuck. Don't tell my grandma." I laughed, trying to make light of the situation, but she didn't laugh.
Silence.
"I'm really sorry. You strong as fuck." I meant that.
"Fuck you, Buddha!" She yelled and stormed back out the door. I was on her ass.
"Man, I said I'm sorry. I fucked up." I admitted. I thought when you said sorry the other person was supposed to forgive you.

Splash....

Aaliyah dived into the pool. She swam in a circle underwater. When I caught on that she was trying to avoid me, I wasn't having it. A nigga kicked off his shoes, socks, and shirt. I stripped down into my Ethika boxers and bolted in the pool too. I went under the water and grabbed her by the waist, pulling her up with me.

Her eyes were bloodshot red. When I saw her lips quiver, that shit made my chest sting.

"I'm sorry, alright?"

She plunged back in the water and swam away from me. I wasn't letting her go. By the time she made it to the wall, I was on her. I snagged her by the arm, pulling her around to face me.

"How can I make it up to you?" I was so close I could kiss her, but I was scared. This girl had me jumping in pools after her.

"It's so much deeper than you and your rude ass assumptions." She spoke just above a whisper, but I could still hear her voice crack.

"I know, but me being an asshole ain't making shit any better."

There was a moment of silence. I may as well put it all out there.

"I knew I should have snatched you up at the club, made you mine, and you wouldn't have to go through half of the shit you

went through. The other half, I would've been there with you every step of the way."
I didn't know where that shit was coming from. My heart hurt for her, knowing that she lost her mom while in prison and had to grieve alone.
"Apology accepted." She tried to walk away again, but this time I pulled her into my arms, wrapping my arms around her body. I held her tightly.

Aaliyah

It was the hug. His muscular arms around me and my head on his toned chest. It was me being vulnerable. My emotions were all over the place. It had been so long since a man held me. So long, since I felt protected. I desired what Buddha was giving me. Even if it was temporary, I needed what he was doing. I needed to feel like someone cared about me, and I wasn't lonely.

 Buddha's hand ran up and down my back. I wasn't sure if he knew what he was doing, but the girl between my legs was feeling some kind of way. Her little ass was jumping. I could feel my warm juices seeping from my hotbox.

"I got you. I got you, cupcake."

Did this man just give me a pet name? No. Did he just tell me he had me?

"Yeah, I said it."

Now he was reading minds.

"You will be alright. I promise not to let another nigga hurt you."

I pulled away and looked up at him. He gave me a half-smile.

Why did he do that? I raised up on tiptoes and planted a kiss on his lips. Buddha pulled back, but I didn't care. I wanted what I believed I needed.

"Stop." He said when I tried to kiss him again.

"What if I don't wanna stop?" I reached into his boxers and almost fainted. Buddha was hard as a rock and his dick was so gotdamn big.

"Aaliyah, stop." He moved back. "I want you but not like this, not while you are all emotional and shit."

I chuckled. I was pissed. I knew what I wanted. I wanted him to fuck me.

"So now I'm emotional? Get the fuck out." I yelled. I was pissed. I didn't care how my actions were making me look either.

Buddha grabbed me by both of my arms. Gazing into my eyes, my body got hotter than an oven.

"Watch your mouth before I give you what you want."

I yanked away. In one swift motion, I took off my two-piece. That nigga's eyes were big as saucers. However, not as big as his dick.

"Fuck it." Buddha mumbled. He took off his boxers and walked up to me. That nigga lifted me up effortlessly. I wrapped my legs around his waist and hungrily took his mouth into mine.

Next thing I knew, I was being tossed on the bed. Buddha was on top of me. He rubbed his tip up and down my clit. I could hear my pussy making swish sounds.

"Ohh." I scooted back. The nigga must've forgotten I hadn't had none in years, plus he was much bigger than any man I had ever been with.

"I'm sorry." He kissed me all over my neck and then back to my lips. Inch by inch, he eased in me.
"Fuck, Aaliyah." He moaned in my ear. Buddha entered me and we both let out a blissful moan. That man sexed my mind, body and soul and that shit scared me.

"Buddha, you got to go. Joy and your uncle will be here." I said covering up in a sheet. He was still lying in bed. He opened his eyes and looked at me.
"You putting me out?"
Looking at the floor, I responded.
"This shouldn't have happened. Please leave. I got too much going on. This should not have happened."
"Why? I told you I got you."
"I don't need you to have me. Damn, can you leave?" I snapped.

Buddha was looking at me like I was crazy. I prayed he didn't slap me. On the other hand, say some mean shit that would hurt my feelings.

"Aaliyah, once you gave me that pussy ain't no turning back. I've wanted you since I saw you at the club. You are mine now. I'm going to let you deal with your emotions. Don't make me mad. It will be your fault if I get out here acting up. I don't want you at the club. That's all I'm saying." Buddha got dressed. He kissed me on my lips and left.
 The man had just put claims on me.
I fell back onto the bed. Confused. I was disappointed because I allowed my emotions to get the best of me. No matter how sexy he was and no matter how badly I wanted him to sex me up, I should've known better. I wasn't ready.

"He pulled out a Glock with an extendo clip."

<u>Jersey</u>

"Damn, bitch. Swallow that shit. Fuck." Head back and mouth open, imagination elsewhere while Karen called herself deep throating my dick. Don't get me wrong, Karen could suck dick, but Macho was in a league of his own. That muthafucka gobbled a dick so gotdamn good a nigga toes be Crip walking, hands throwing up sign language, and mind on making a nigga his main bitch.

Nah, I wasn't a gay nigga though, so that would never happen. I just liked getting my dick sucked by dudes and from time to time, I might get some nigga pussy. I wasn't into it like that. Tokyo got turned on by me doing that, so sometimes I would let her have her way.

She never let me sample Macho's pussy. Only Parker's. I think she was scared that me, and Macho would have relations behind her back.

 Anyway, back to this bitch. I'd been fucking with Karen for a few months. I was riding through her hood one day, saw her and Jam getting into it. Since I didn't like the nigga no more or his bitch ass crew, I stopped and got all up in his business. I wanted him to say something, and, on my momma, I was going to rock his ass. Fuck a white boy.

I got out of the car right where they argued and posted up against my car. Like what? Karen was crying about him only keeping their daughter so he wouldn't have to pay child support. Jam told her since she was back on that shit, he was never giving her back and to go get a job.

"That's how you do our black queens?" I teased.

"Says the nigga who let his baby's momma take his case. Fuck out of here, lame."

I ran up on the nigga and he pulled out a Glock with an extendo clip. With a smirk, he aimed it at me. I wasn't scary, but I wasn't stupid either. I let him have that.

"That's what I thought, bitch." He spat before jumping in his Dodge Charger and burning rubber, leaving skid marks and two muthafuckas who wanted revenge behind.

"That's what happens when you fuck with lame-ass white boys. And, to think I had a crush on you all these years. Got that nigga out here making you look stupid." I jumped back in my car and left.

I knew what I was doing. I waited before I got at her. All I had to do was throw her some money, fuck her, and let her get high in peace. In return, I could push work out of her house and get in her head. Karen would eventually help me get rid of Jam and his crew with no help from the police.

You see what I'm saying. Almost forgot this bitch was sucking my dick. I grabbed Karen by the hair and fucked her in the mouth until I nutted down her throat.

I jumped up from the couch. She laid back on the floor, butt naked with her legs wide open.

"I got stuff to do." I told her, pulling up my jeans. I reached in my pocket and peeled off two big faces from my stack. I sat it on the couch.

"Damn. I can't get no dick?"

"Not right now. Hey, where that nigga Jam momma stay?"

"Really. You are thinking about him?" She stood up and put her hands on her hips.

"Alright, I'm out. I'll be back to get my shit. You let him take care of you."

"Where is this coming from?" She looked stunned.

"Don't worry about it."

Mind games were a muthafucka. I headed out the door, ignoring her plea to talk. I wasn't planning on making a move on Jam and their crew just yet, but when I did, I wanted to have all I needed to make the shake-up easy.

I jumped in my car and saw I had five missed calls from Tokyo. The text she sent said 9-1-1. I hoped she and Dream were okay.

I immediately called back.

"What's up? Are you good? Where is the baby?"

"She is right here. We are at my momma's house."

"What's up?"

"The tenant called." She paused before speaking again. "You- know- who- called."

"Ok, who called? I don't know who you-know-who is." The fuck.

"The tenant called and said a lady by the name of Ms. Monroe came by and said that she was in her home. She asked for me, and she gave her my number. She asked her questions and her old stupid ass answered. Then she said she would move back in soon and the tenant would have to find a place to stay."

"What the fuck you think going on?"

"Somebody playing. Aaliyah can't be out. Ignore that shit."

"I'm going to call Parker to see what he can find out. See if she's out."

"Man, that girl ain't out." She replied, thinking it couldn't be possible.

Deep down, in a way I hoped she got a miracle. Aaliyah was a good person.

"I gotta call you back." I hung up.

What if she was out? The shit would be crazy. I didn't even want to think about it.

Another call came through, and it was the young homeboy Pop.

"Sup." I answered.

"I heard Kash and them will be at club Highland tonight. Let's pull up."

"Hell, yeah."

I hadn't seen the nigga since we had a meeting with Big O. His pops, Mr. LA was on the phone a couple of years ago.

First O claimed we were taking over the streets – the east, west, south, and north. I was down. Then he changed the shit up. Like he was scared of L.A.

I mean, we were making money staying on our side of town, but I wanted it all. Kash, Jam, and their crew were eating way better. I didn't like that. I had a trick, though.

A few tricks. Watch this!

The youngster and I talked a little more. We hung up. I headed over to the house Tokyo and her sister used to live in together. Right after the baby shower, we rented it out. Tokyo's idea, but it was a good one. Too many people knew where we stayed.

"The muthafuckas were going to pay."

Aaliyah

I couldn't stop smiling as I stood in the mirror looking like a brand-new woman. Jon Jon, Ms. Myers's son, flat ironed my hair. He had it bone straight with a part in the middle. My hair passed my bra strap. Joy brought her makeup bag to do my makeup, but she didn't know that I was a beast with the makeup brush. I did my makeup so good she had me to do hers and her friend Rina's.
"You should do this as a side-hustle." Rina suggested.
"Thanks. Good idea." I countered.

Tonight I put on a one-piece skin tight black bodysuit, which was see-through at the top. To make my outfit pop, I wore a neon-yellow colored bra to match my neon-yellow and black six-inch ankle strap stiletto heels. I was so cute I could make the deacon of a church forget his bible scriptures. I checked myself out in the full-length mirror and blew myself a kiss.
 "You cute friend, here." Joy said, handing me a glass.
"Thanks. You too." Joy wore black booty shorts, a red bra, and a black blazer. On her feet were a pair of red and black ones. Rina

wore a white maxi dress that flowed down to her feet.

 Me, Rina, and Joy talked while having a couple of drinks. The entire time, I was thinking of Buddha and how good he made me feel. I was so glad he left. I didn't want anyone in my business. Believe it or not, I felt bad that I put him out.

"You know who I haven't seen?" Rina said. We were headed to Joy's truck.

"Who?" Joy asked.

"Buddha big dick ass." She giggled.

 I almost spit out my drink. No the hell she didn't just brag about a dick I just got through screwing. I gave her the once over while cutting my eyes before climbing in the back seat. So, he fucked this bitch. I chuckled to myself. He probably fucked all of Joy's friends.

I caught Joy looking at me through the rearview mirror.

"You want another drink?" She asked.

"Yesss. I wanna get faded. I deserve it. But where's my nigga Buddha." Rina was doing too much for me.

"I'll have one." I cut in.

"Girl, Buddha should be the least of your worries. That shit is ancient. I can't believe you are still thinking about that boy." Joy retorted.

She handed us each a red cup before pulling off.

"Big dicks never get old." She laughed. My lips had a straight line. That shit wasn't funny.

 Listening to Rina, I was so turned off. I was glad when Joy turned up the music.

Looking down at my phone, I was surprised that I had a text. Ms. Myers and Joy's phone numbers were saved. I opened the phone. To see who the number was.

Unknown: I thought I asked you not to go to the club tonight.

My heart thumped when I read the text. I would have been flattered had I not just found out he was community dick.

Me: How did you get my number? You are giving me stalker vibes.

Unknown: Tell my aunt to take you home.

Me: No.

Unknown: Bet

We pulled in VIP. I was feeling good off the fruity drink Joy made me. After fixing our makeup and spraying on more perfume. We gassed up the car and headed to the club. I was so glad we didn't have to stand in the long ass line. Joy walked straight up to the front. Whatever she told the security, it granted us access.

 When we walked in, I felt a little nervous because there were so many people in the building, something I was no longer used to. Rina and Joy bobbed their heads to the music as we made our way to wherever we were going. Maybe I should have stayed home. The last time I went to the club was with my best friend. I missed Val. I knew she missed me, too. The only reason I hadn't tried to reach her was because I was ashamed. I wanted to get myself together first, but seeing Rina and Joy made me want my friend.

 Our first stop was the bar. The bartender placed three shots on the counter. Each one of us took the shot.

"I got a table. Let's go. "Joy said. She was in the front then me and then Rina.

We were in VIP, chilling. I liked it better on the upper level. I grabbed a bottle of water and stood over the banister, watching the crowd. Looking towards the stairs, my eyes widened. Buddha was climbing the stairs two at a time headed to VIP, something told me he was about to act stupid.

I continued to look over the banister. My plan was to pay him no mind.

'Damn he looks good,' I thought. A few moments later, I could feel someone standing behind me. The DJ switched from Cardi B to Usher. Buddha wrapped his arms around me, lightly rocking from side to side. In my ear, he whispered.

"I wasn't planning on coming to the club tonight, but you are hardheaded. I asked you not to come."

I didn't know what his problem was, but he was not my man.

I shook my head. "You are not my man. I need you to move your arms from around me. You are messing with any action I may have."

"What?" He put his lips to my ear.

"Go find Rina. Now move." I tried to break from him, but he wouldn't let me. I swear he was such a bully.

"Girl, I ain't thinking about her. I got who I want."

I didn't bother to respond. I allowed him to invade my space. I didn't want to admit it, but I felt protected in his arms.

A little while later, Joy came over. She gave us a knowing look and smirked. Rina was shocked. She put one hand over her mouth. "I didn't know. I apologize. That was old." She whispered.

I gave her a reverse nod and looked at Joy. "We are about to go to the third level. Just saw a few friends. You good?"

"Yeah."

"We about to go." I heard Buddha tell her. Joy looked at me to confirm.

Forget it, I thought I had been out long enough and plus I wasn't comfortable.

"Thanks for the invite." I told her. She hugged me and she and Rina walked off. Buddha kissed the side of my face before grabbing my hand and escorting me out the club. I didn't know what to think or how to feel about whatever it was that Buddha thought he and I had.

It wasn't a surprise that Buddha was popular. So many people were coming up to him speaking and giving him fist bumps, I was surprised we made it out of the club. Even in the parking lot a few chicks made it their business to call his name.
"I like you, cupcake." He said. I looked at him and then back straight ahead.
He hit a button on his key fob and I heard the engine roar on his Dodge Charger.
"I'm hungry." I told him.
"Ok." He shut my door. When he got in the car, he asked me what I wanted to eat. I told him tacos. I hadn't eaten them in forever.
"No, the fuck-" I said, more to myself. I rolled my window down just to make sure I wasn't seeing things. Across the way were Jersey and Tokyo. She stood in front of him, his arm wrapped around her waist, and someone was taking their picture. They looked like the perfect couple.
"What's wrong, cupcake?" He leaned over to see where I was looking.

"Oh, that nigga Jersey. I'm about to beat his ass." Before I could respond, he jumped out of the car. I kicked off my heels and jumped out with him.

Buddha was already up on Jersey. With a balled fist, he hit him with a sharp blow to the head. He crumpled to the ground, unconscious. He lifted his foot and violently stomped him out. Now it was my turn. I ran up to Tokyo. She threw the first punch but missed. I punched her like we were in a boxing ring. She swung back, but those weak ass licks were no match for the beat down I was putting on her. I was bigger, swifter, angrier, and had been wanting to beat her ass for a while. She tripped on a sidewalk curb and fell. I pounced on her, grabbed her throat, and squeezed until she couldn't breathe.

Suddenly, I felt someone snatch me up off of her. It was Buddha.

"You gon' kill that bitch. Let's bounce before someone calls 'the boys.' I ain't trying to get locked up." He said. He grabbed my hand and led me away. I looked back towards Tokyo. She had gotten up and was walking over to help her man up. Our eyes locked. Her face went from shocked to mad.

"You gonna regret this, bitch!" She yelled.

"Only thing I regret is that I didn't kill yo' bitch ass!" I backfired.

Buddha burned rubber out of the parking lot.

We road in silence for a little bit before he spoke.

"I see you had your man's back."

"Whatever."

"Oh, so I'm not your man?"

"Nope."

"You still hungry?"

"Yeah."

I sat back thinking about Tokyo with Jersey and how they were raising my baby together. Sadness tried to take over, but I shook it off.

"I swear they will regret ever fucking me over." I mumbled.

The muthafuckas were going to pay.

"Buddha, I think you should go home." I looked straight ahead. I could feel him staring at me.

"So, you really not fucking with me?" He snapped. I didn't like his tone. I turned and faced him. Granted, this man was so fine to me. The sex was amazing, I just couldn't see myself getting involved with anyone right then.

"Didn't you just see my sister and my man together?" I snapped.

"Your man? You calling that nigga your man?" He asked through clenched teeth.

"I didn't mean it like that. I really didn't. It just came out like that."

"That wasn't no fucking slip up. If that's who you want, then go for it. I ain't never thirsty for no silly ass broad."

Wham!

I tried to slap him so hard that Google maps wouldn't be able to find his ass. He was so disrespectful. I knew he was mad, but still, he couldn't just say whatever it was he wanted to say.

I watched as he massaged his jaw with his tongue. I was waiting for an apology.

"Get out of my car, Aaliyah." He looked at me. The frown on his face made me sad. Ok, the truth was, I did like Buddha, but I wasn't sure if it was because I needed it. In need of feeling loved. In need of feeling like there was someone on earth who cared about me and because I didn't know if my feelings were real, I was going to keep my distance.

"I sure will get out. From this day forward, don't say shit to me." I hopped out of the car. He jumped out right behind me.

"I don't give a fuck. I ain't gotta say shit to you. You ain't the only bitch out here with good pussy."

I stopped in my tracks. When I turned around, he was right up on me.

"So you calling me out of my name and putting me out of your car?"

I was all up in his face. I felt so weak under his gaze.

"I apologize. I will never call you out of your name again. I ain't going to say shit to you again. Have a nice life."

My heart dropped. I blinked several times trying to digest what he said. My mind was telling me that he needed to go. I had no room in my life to entertain him. However, my heart was telling me he was who I needed, even if it was only for a season.

Buddha shocked the hell out of me when he leaned in and covered my mouth with his. A light moaned escaped my lips when I tasted his meaty tongue. My arms went around his neck. I could feel my juices flowing from my center, and we shared an electrifying kiss. When he pulled away, I could have sworn I saw fireworks. He gave me another peck. As he pulled away, my arms dropped to my sides. I stared at him hoping he would take me inside and fuck me before he left. Damn, he knew he was handsome.

Buddha threw up the dueces at me before walking away. In disbelief, I watched as he hopped in his car and pulled off. I was floored. He really dissed me. I didn't turn to go inside until he was out of sight. Maybe I was hoping he would come back.

I happened to look up at Ms. Myer's house. I saw her looking out the bedroom window. She gave a smile and closed the curtain.

That night, I tossed and turned until I eventually fell asleep. I was wishing Buddha was there with me. I wanted to feel him. Oooh his sex was so good. If I wasn't in the situation I was in, I probably would've entertained the idea of us being one. When I finally went to sleep, his fine ass was in my dreams. He surprised me with flowers. He then put a rag around my eyes and told me he had a surprise for me. I was cheering big time.

Ring ring ring... The cheap ass prepaid ringer was so loud. I was already a light sleeper. It woke me up.

"Hello." I answered eagerly. Deep down, I wanted it to be Buddha telling me to open the door.

"Aaliyah, where are y'all at? Buddha still with you?" Joy said in a panic that caused me to wake up.

"No, he dropped me off."
I was scared to ask what was wrong.

"Oh my God. Please God, don't let it be him. I need you to go wake up my momma. Tell her to call me! Please!" Joy hung up.
I jumped up from the bed and dressed in record time. I could feel my heart beat in my throat.

"I begged God."
<u>Rina</u>

My oversized designer shades covered my eyes. I wasn't only trying to keep the sun out, but I was trying to keep my cover. I didn't want to run into anyone. The only reason I went to the party was because Kash was going to be there, and he was who I came back to see. It was time for him to share my truths and apologize for not telling him about his son.

 At the club last night, I saw a couple of O's workers and tried to creep out before I was noticed.

 My heels clicked against the pavement as I made my way into the establishment. To be safe, I suggested that we meet in the city of Malibu. He wanted to know why, but I told him that I had my reasons, and it was for safety.

"I have a reservation for two. I would love to sit in the back." I said to the waitress.
"Sure, no problem. Is there another party here?"
"No, but his name is Kash. He should be coming, but I will sit now."
"Of course." She escorted me to my seat. It was right in the back by an exit. I could view the side of the restaurant and half of the parking lot from where I sat. What I

liked about the place besides the food was that the windows were dark. You could only see out. People couldn't see in.

I decided not to have anything to drink besides water. I didn't have an appetite, but I ordered a few appetizers just in case Kash wanted some. I prayed so much last night, I even called and asked Ms. Myers to pray with me. My prayer was that Kash would understand my situation and forgive me for my wrong.

I had just sipped from my glass of water when I felt a touch on my shoulder. I tensed up. Pulling my hat further down my head, I slowly turned around and looked at Nita. Nita and my dad were messing around before I left. My heart dropped. My stomach balled up in a knot. I didn't even have a weapon on me. It was at that moment I knew I should have allowed Joy Ann to come with me. If push came to shove, I was going to scream bloody mercy in that muthafucka.

The tears in Nita's eyes surprised me. I wondered if my dad had something to do with her tears, maybe she found out he was fucking her scandalous ass friend.

"Don't think I'm drunk because I am not. I'm a little tipsy, but I am not drunk." She stated. I didn't respond. Nita forcefully wiped the fresh tears that ran down her face.

"I ain't no saint. I have flaws just like the next woman. I did some things that I am not proud of in my life, but one thing I can tell you is that I have always been a loyal person to those I love and care about. What happened to me is my fault. It's my fault because I took all the signs for granted."

I took a deep breath and let it out. Nita did not know she was speaking to me. Something told me she was chatting about my father. I bet he hurt her, just like he did my mother.

"I should've run. The clues were there. He never took full responsibility for his actions. He continuously cheated with different women. I even welcomed other women in the bedroom, and he still went behind my back and slept with my friend and others. I wanted that man to see that I was the one he needed in his life so bad that I went against my morals. I ignored the muthafucking signs. When his wife left him and turned up dead, he blamed her. He said, If she didn't leave, then she would still be alive."

"Only a heartless person would say that. I should have known that muthafucka was crazy. He tried to choke the life out of me when I told him that he was pimping his daughter instead of being a father." She revealed. For some reason, I felt sorry for her. As a woman, I felt her pain. I could relate to the hurt that she felt.

My eyes fluttered. I instantly placed my hand over my chest.

"I'm sorry, baby. Please don't ever lose yourself over a man. I did and fucked around and got AIDS." She shook her head and walked away.
 Wow, Nita had AIDS.
"Ms. Nita, did my father give you AIDS." I sympathetically asked out of curiosity. I took my hat and shades off.
 Nita stopped in her tracks. She turned around. Her eyes narrowed in at me before they grew wide. She looked up at the ceiling.
"Oh my Jesus!" She yelped. Looking behind her nervously scared me. Nita rushed to me. She grabbed me by my hand.
"Rina, Rina.. just last night I asked God what I am to do with the information I found out and here you are."
"Did my father give you AIDS?" I wanted to know, revisiting the question again.

"Oh, baby." Her voice cracked. Nita pulled me into her arms. She held me so tight like she never wanted to let me go.

"Rina, I am so sorry, I have to tell you something." She pulled away.

"It can't be here."

"Tell me. Did my father give you AIDS?"

"Yes, it was him. He admitted it. I don't think I'm the only one that he gave it to. Your father is evil. Can we go somewhere to talk?"

I stood there in disbelief. A man who, I believe, was the manager came over and asked us if everything was okay. I gave him a head nod. Then took a seat. Nita sat across from me.

"I am leaving town in the morning. What I am about to tell you can get me into a lot of trouble. I don't care. I begged God for a sign and seeing you, I have the sign, Rina." She grabbed my hand.

"Your father had your mother killed for the insurance money."

"Wait...wait. What did you say?" I was beginning to panic.

"I don't have proof, but I overheard him on the phone, and I still didn't leave him." She put her head down.

I jumped up from the table and took off running out of the restaurant.

Right game, wrong bitch.

<u>Tokyo</u>

I woke up the next morning sore as hell. My fat stupid sister caught me slipping and tried me. I fell, and that's when her heavy ass jumped on top of me. I could barely move. That's why I didn't feel bad about what happened to the dude she was with last night. He got what he deserved. Now, I bet he won't try that bullshit with nobody else. Jersey was laying in the bed with me. He had an ice pack over his black eye and had been throwing up blood all night long. I hated Aaliyah!

Dream woke up and came into our room.

"Mommy, I'm hungry." She said.

My daughter was so cute and looked just like her daddy.

"Okay, I'll get you some breakfast."

Jersey moaned out in pain and rolled over on his side. With my cellphone in hand, I checked it to see if I had any missed calls. Sure enough, I had three missed calls from my mother. I also had a text message from her.

Momma: Girl, I found out Warren has AIDS. I'm at the doctor's office. I keep throwing up, and I'm sick as hell. I just took a rapid test. I'm waiting for the results to come back now. Please pray for me.

I stepped outside onto the front porch to keep Jersey out of my business. I needed to speak to my mother privately. I knew she shouldn't have been fucking around with Warren's dirty dick. My hand shook from nervousness. I dialed her number back. She didn't answer, so I hung up. I rubbed up and down the side of my neck as I thought about Aaliyah choking me out.

I promised myself that the next time we saw each other, I would sock her right in the face. Jersey was my man. I wasn't letting her take my man or my baby away from me. Right game, wrong bitch. Taking her man and baby was sweet but getting revenge on that hoe will be even sweeter. Hmph. I will stop at nothing to get her back. PERIODT!

To Be Continued....

I thank you for reading. More titles by
Alana's Book Line are on amazon or
www.inspiringhoodauthor.com

www.ingramcontent.com/pod-product-compliance
Lightning Source LLC
Chambersburg PA
CBHW072011170726
47999CB00014B/1519